— 2000.

Pomegranate Season

Carolyn Polizzotto

Pomegranate Season

Carolyn Polizzotto

FREMANTLE ARTS CENTRE PRESS

First published 1998 by
FREMANTLE ARTS CENTRE PRESS
193 South Terrace (PO Box 320), South Fremantle
Western Australia 6162.
www.facp.iinet.net.au

Consultant Editor Wendy Jenkins.
Designer Marion Duke.
Production Manager Cate Sutherland.
Cover and internal photographs by Graham Miller.

Typeset by Fremantle Arts Centre Press
and printed by South Wind Production, Singapore.

National Library of Australia
Cataloguing-in-Publication data:

Polizzotto, Carolyn, 1948–.
Pomegranate Season.

ISBN 1 86368 226 0.

I. Title.

A823.3

A
artswa

The State of Western Australia has made an investment in
this project through the Department for the Arts.

for Lorenzo

... it can happen that an author, a woman, comes too close to a woman to get to make her acquaintance, in the sense of discovering her still unknown. And thus, through familiarity, she misses her. What to do? A trip around the world to make an entrance from the other side, this time as a stranger.

Hélène Cixous
in *'Coming to Writing' and Other Essays*

Part One
Autumn

17 May

Autumn is my favourite season. In Perth, though, the summers are long and the winters short. Only a hair's breadth divides them.

So I have to be alert for fleeting pleasures. Frost on the grass is one; turning leaves are another. Echoes of full-blown autumns from places far away. But the frost is no more than a faint sheen at first light. It doesn't last long enough for you to see your footprints in it. And there are no drifts of fallen leaves to shuffle through.

I'm more of a winter person now.

18 May

Autumn in our garden is heralded by the pomegranates ripening. This is the only sign that anything's changing; and it happens far too soon, when the sun is still fierce. I scurry out to pick a few, but it's a chore, squinting up into the branches, stretching up against the blinding light. The rest are eaten by the tree rats. They scoop them out completely, cleanly; it's endearing, almost. The man at the Council won't have them called tree rats: they're as bad as the river rats, as far as he's concerned; but locally it's an important distinction. We like to think of our long-tailed rats as quaint local fauna, and since they refuse to be exterminated, it's probably a good idea. Our cat Sebastian used to keep them under control, but then Missy, the dog, arrived, and banned him from the garden. Even Missy was a reasonably good ratter, but she's got too old for it, so there's a midden of empty lemon rinds at the back of the wood heap as well.

They don't bother me now, as they would have when the children were small. Keeping clean was hard enough without rats to worry about. I was always on edge about the mess. With teenagers I'm more relaxed, not to say slovenly. The dirt and I co-exist. I feel like an empty rind myself, sometimes.

Apart from the pomegranates, the only other sign of autumn in this garden is the Virginia creeper. I watch it from the windows, determined that this year I'll catch it turning, but it remains resolutely green as long as I'm looking. Each year I give up in the end, and turn away, and then in the blink of an eye it goes to red. Today the leaves are yellow and orange, almost bronze.

Because the years have started to pass too quickly for me, I've decided to plant bulbs as a way of slowing them down. This diary is to be a record of my successes and failures, so that next time I'll get everything right. The last time I tried to plant them was sixteen years ago. We'd just moved to this house, and I was full of enthusiasm. The children were small and it was the sort of thing you could do with them, a way of passing the time, as long as you never expected to get anything finished. I planted nasturtiums, which flourished, and daffodils, which never appeared. Not one, not ever.

Time seemed to stand completely still then. I suppose the children took all of it; they needed it to grow in. Month after endless month, they took, and maybe there wasn't enough left over for the daffodils.

19 May

Today is Sunday, and I've been able to spend the whole day in the garden. Luke's away at camp for the weekend, Laurie's gone to work to do corrections, and only Mark is at home with me. I'd like to describe a day of colourful plantings but I spent it raking leaves and trimming edges. I transplanted a frangipani which has never flowered to a sunnier spot outside the wall. And I battled with the buffalo grass, which has taken an instant liking to bulb fertiliser, and is making lightning strikes into the bulb beds. (Meanwhile, the sandy wastes of our verge, which are supposed to be turning into a blue-green buffalo carpet, are as bare as ever.)

I planted seventy-five daffodils and jonquils in those beds last month. The daffodils are 'King Alfred' and 'Pheasant's Eye', and the jonquils are 'Paperwhite' and 'Grand Monarch'. So far there's no sign of any of them, but the 'McCartney' and 'Albertine' roses in the same place have each put on half a metre's growth.

I've noticed another sign of autumn. The sun has dropped away to the north, and that makes an extraordinary difference to the light. The rays seem much longer, and diffused, so that it's hard to believe this is the same sun which was burning directly overhead only yesterday. The leaves of the trees are now lit from below in the early morning and late afternoon. The garden is like a stage set.

20 May

This garden is tiny by Western Australian standards. It's really only two courtyards, linked by a brick pathway which has crabapple trees growing alongside it. But last night, before going to sleep, I wandered through it in my mind, thinking over the work I'd done during the day; and it was as though I was walking through the world. I didn't get to the end of it before falling asleep. For the last year or so, I haven't been able to settle at night. I find myself getting up to check the boys' breathing.

I want to plant dichondra in between the sandstone paving. I've also bought a viola, with an exotic name, to plant in the terracotta duck. The duck was bought as a joke, and set on one of the gateposts, but the Argentine ants adored it (elevated position, excellent ventilation) and made a home there. The point was reached where they took over management of the gate, because they didn't like being disturbed when it was opened, and firm action was necessary. Nothing worked, Argentine ants being what they are, and finally we had to take the duck down.

I was embarrassed to find how fond I'd grown of it. I've noticed this before, with kitsch things. It's a risk to buy them, even as a joke, because they have a way of endearing themselves to you and then you can't bear to throw them out. I'm trying the duck on the front verandah, near the door, where the violas — 'The Czar', they're called — will get the winter sun. 'Semi-shade', the label says, of their preferred position, but in our garden there's no such thing. The choice is either direct sun — not to be taken lightly, in Perth — or under the trees, where all is deepest gloom.

22 May

Always, in this season, I think of my old friend Judy in London, waiting for warmer weather, while I am here, longing for the cold.

What to cook? When Mark was a baby, and starting on solids, I used to make him chocolate mousse, and apple charlotte. Little custards. The idea was to train his palate *from the outset*; and I loved cooking, then. He wouldn't touch them, of course; tinned baby food was all he'd eat. Now everyone clamours for chocolate mousse, and I can't be bothered making it.

24 May

It's taken me until today to make a start with the dichondra. The earth between the paving stones was packed so hard that I needed to go back to the plant nursery to buy some potting mix to replace it with. Then I found builders' sand below, and that had to be dug out. It was noon before I took a close look at the dichondra, to find that the half-dozen punnets I've bought are actually seed plug containers, with twelve plugs of dichondra seedlings in each.

This is one of the difficulties of beginning new projects in a garden which you've already established, and which, while it is far from spectacular, more or less looks after itself. The disruption is hardly worth the effort. Left to themselves, the paving stones and the gaps between them were invisible beneath the lantanas. Now I've cut the lantanas back so that I can get at the paving stones, dirt and sand are lying in heaps everywhere, and the plugs of dichondra, planted a regulation fifteen centimetres apart (those few I've done), look as though they were ordered by the Red Queen. Bulb planting was about as near as I wanted to get to painting the roses red, in this climate.

My back is aching; and my legs are stiff from kneeling. We've had crisp, bright, cold days all week and the weather is to continue fine, so perhaps I'll regain my enthusiasm over the weekend. Gardening is slow work; it won't be hurried, and I simply don't have the right temperament. I want results, and I want them *now*.

The one bright spot has been the violas. When I went to plant them, I found that each had produced two flowers! The blooms are white and fluffy, about the size of a violet, but being double they are more noticeable.

25 May

Part of the reason for my hurry is that this mild weather will be over so soon. The autumn days — and they have been truly autumnal this past week — will give way to wind and rain before we know it. This morning, for example, though only for a few minutes, there were some short, sharp gusts of biting south-west wind that came out of nowhere. There will be no more time to garden once the rain comes.

26 May

We built the brick wall only a few years after we came here, and it made such a difference to the garden. On the one hand, the soil near it retained more moisture, and some plants flourished. On the other, there was much less sunshine.

We have a dog staying with us. Bibi is a Jack Russell terrier, whose owner, my friend Irene, has gone away for the weekend. Bibi must be about four now, and she's very lively, making me realise how Missy is ageing. When Bibi was a puppy, and wanted to play with us, Missy would interfere and stop the game. Now that she is an elderly dog, she just watches sorrowfully. She has osteoarthritis in her back legs and has grown very deaf.

The section of wall which faces west is not solid brick, but brick columns interspersed with large panels of green lattice. That part of the garden is overshadowed by a huge Japanese pepper tree. As I write this I realise that the thrumming of the bees in its branches, which seemed to go on all through the summer months, has stopped.

Planting dichondra is a task for giants. I still haven't cleaned up. I pruned two of the 'Iceberg' roses, to make a change from stooping, as well as the winter jasmine with which they are locked in perpetual combat. Those cut branches need clearing away as well. In winter, I am told, the dichondra will take off *like wildfire*.

27 May

There is still no rain, and this year is now officially the fourth driest on record. Rain was forecast yesterday afternoon, but the only sign of it was a greyish-blue haze in the afternoon, and none fell.

I woke this morning to golden light reflecting off the leaves of the giant flame tree next door. The Virginia creeper is copper and crimson, with only one or two yellowy-green leaves remaining. This year I've watched it turn.

I'm shut indoors with my work deadlines.

29 May

Working for yourself leaves space to pursue other passions, like gardening. But that's not the best thing about it. The best thing, the very best thing, is being able to work in your nightie, all day if you want to. (And tracksuit pants in colder weather.)

The worst thing is the isolation. It can become hard to make yourself go out.

30 May

The weeping mulberry turns much later than the Virginia creeper. The leaves at the bottom of each branch are now lemon yellow, and there are spaces between them so that each leaf is clearly itself. Against today's grey sky, they look delicate and wintry. After the summer we've had, it is life-giving to record every shade of variation in the light. (According to the newspapers, we'd been nine months without a cool day, until last week.)

31 May

There has been a period of a couple of years where I've measured out the days with waiting. Waiting for Luke to get himself ready for school. Waiting for the mail to come. Waiting for Mark to get up and go to university on the days when he has a late start. Waiting for him to come home on the days he finishes early. Waiting until it's cool enough to take the dog for a walk in the evening.

A lot of my waiting is done in the car. Outside schools, outside sports grounds.

Outside movie theatres. I take a book, and, if I remember, my reading glasses as well. I even take a cup of tea and a sandwich. The car becomes a dwelling place: more comfortable, almost, than the house. Certainly more private. I do a lot of waiting in the car.

But I've also been waiting *in case*. I've waited in case Mark might want lunch. In case Luke gets sick at school. Even on weekends, I wait, because there might be a phone call from someone who's got themselves stuck, and wants a lift home.

Part Two
Winter

1 June

It rained heavily during the night, and I woke to find the sky grey and the ground wet; or rather the brick paths were wet. There was no sign of moisture on the earth, because the water had soaked in so fast.

There's a delicious sense of pervertedness about rejoicing in a sunless sky. Is it too wet to garden?

2 June

I did get out yesterday afternoon, to finish planting the dichondra. I also cleared the high grass away from the arum lilies in the back garden. They come up each year by themselves.

In any other year, I'd have to leave the house more often. I'd be doing interviews, or going through archives. Instead I'm in between, finishing off one project (a company history that's taken several years), and starting another: a site history of a group of shops in Cottesloe. The big history is all but complete. I'm just giving a final check to the typescript, before getting it bound. With the site history, I'm still feeling my way.

Jo Trevelyan is the inspiration behind it. She wants to commission some sort of artwork which will alert passers-by to the fact that people have lived and worked in this well-to-do coastal suburb, midway between Perth and Fremantle, for well over a century. The site is a group of shops in Napoleon Street, and my job is to provide the background. It's an exciting brief. Jo and I have always had a rapport, but now a friendship has developed, and we get together every couple of weeks. About one meeting in five is a work meeting.

I need to make a start. It's like choosing where to hit the water when you dive. I have to read what's already been published (which, like checking the typescript, I can do at home), and to decide at what point to plunge into the unknown world of the handwritten records.

It leaves plenty of time for gardening; and plenty — too much, perhaps — for reflection.

3 June

My mother's bridal bouquet was of arum lilies, and I had always associated them with her wedding portrait, which is not a flattering one. She looks large-nosed and awkward in the sepia photograph, and so do they. Their renaissance for me began about five years ago, when I saw one drawn in profile. It was done like an engineering design, showing those extraordinary curves, and since then I've waited eagerly for them each year.

There are little blue flowers growing alongside the arum lilies, which come up each year too. I'd always assumed they were weeds. On my recent bulb-buying expeditions, however, I've seen them glowingly portrayed on packets. They've turned out to be bluebells, and I'm taking them seriously now.

When we first came to this house we found slipper orchids under the robinia tree. We were fairly new to Western Australia and assumed that they must grow everywhere. Like the arum lilies and the bluebells, they appeared each year, unwatered, unfertilised, making no fuss; and we thought they always would. But the wall ended their life. Whether it was the trampling of the bricklayers' feet, or the shadow it cast, they never came back. It was years before I even noticed; and years more before I realised what we'd lost.

I've rather overdone the bulb planting. Those I put in today looked moribund, and I don't honestly expect them to come up. They should have been planted by May at the latest, and although it is only the very beginning of June, the weather has definitely turned colder. I'd thought I could fool the bulbs into believing it was still autumn — what difference can a couple of days make, after all? — but they looked quite different from those I planted in April and May: much less fresh, somehow; and some of them had started to sprout, which I seem to remember is a bad sign.

It's a grey day, and there's been some rain. However much I long for this weather, it still saddens me when it comes.

4 June

The robinia tree dominates our garden. Its timber is so dense and hard that, in England, one of its common names is 'the axe-handle tree'. Ours is thirty metres high, with two trunks; a vast, benign presence. It has lost almost all its leaves. Every twig is outlined blackly against an almost white sky. (It was raining in the early hours of the morning.)

The only other tree which approaches the robinia in height is the ornamental fig on the verge. It looks like a young Moreton Bay, but it's not: it's an old *Ficus hillii*, Laurie says. Originating in the rain forests of North Queensland, these were a popular street tree until, with the introduction of underground sewerage systems, their liking for water pipes became a problem. Ours has somehow survived, as has our neighbours' opposite, and their branches meet to form an arch above the road.

For ten days or so, both were full of furious squeaking birds. 'Weddings,' Irene said when she came to collect Bibi, but then she thought of silvereyes. These are a small, fruit-loving bird, with an uncanny ability to tell when something is perfectly ripe. By their combined efforts, they can leave large fruit scooped out very cleanly. Perhaps they, and not rats, have been responsible for the pomegranates. (This doesn't explain the pile of lemon skins near the firewood, though.)

I wonder if it was a silvereye that Laurie pointed out to me a couple of summers ago. We had the lawn sprinkler on the frangipani outside the kitchen window, and this tiny bird was rolling down the long wet leaf, taking flight an instant before it would have hit the ground, and then starting once more from the top. It was so unusual to see a wild bird *playing* like that. The fig's small, brownish-mauve berries, most of them squashed, are carpeting the driveway and the road. The silvereyes have left.

I'm at a loose end, because Luke has just set off with his friend Trevor, to see a movie in town. Luke is sixteen; Trevor's a year older. It's the first time they have gone alone, completely without supervision. His absence gives me about three hours to myself, which I'm not used to on a school holiday. I don't know what to do with the time. It doesn't seem long enough to be of any use.

Three hours used to be so precious. When Luke was a little boy, I'd have someone come in to care for him, one morning a week, from nine till twelve. I'd be wanting to get the most out of my break, and fearful that something would go wrong: either that he'd get sick, or that the babysitter would cancel, both of which happened, often enough. I learned not to plan *too carefully*; not to care *too much*.

When my friend Penny's little girl died suddenly in the night, of a virus which crossed from her lungs to her heart, Penny walked out into her front garden at dawn. First she heard the birds start singing, and then the sun rose; and finally even the paper boy came by, as usual. Penny could not believe that these things could still happen in a world which no longer held her daughter.

For me, with Luke, it was different. The sun simply left the sky. I was in Melbourne, driving home with Laurie's sister, Anna. Luke must have been about six weeks old. It was a sunny day in early March. I'd not said anything to anyone about the niggling doubts that were trickling into the back of my throat.

Mark had been born in Melbourne, a year after we came back from London, and we'd followed the dwindling supply of academic posts to Perth soon afterwards. With our families still living in Melbourne, and a hospital and doctor that I knew, I went back to have my second baby. I'd wanted everything the same as the first time; and everything was, at first. But by the time Luke was six weeks old, I knew that something was different.

In a car, sometimes conversations are possible that aren't elsewhere. Saying the words to Anna, though, that I'd not said to anyone, I felt the sun go in. *Not for years* did I realise that this hadn't actually happened.

5 June

Driving to Claremont along the railway line this afternoon, I was struck by the long, thin shadows across the road. They could have been cast by skyscrapers, rather than Norfolk pines. The low angle of the sun was accentuated by the fact that it was relatively late in the day (about four pm). The winter solstice is less than three weeks away, and then the days will begin to get longer again. I feel cheated of my winter.

It was in this sort of weather that Judy came to stay. She'd not known what clothes to bring and was sceptical of my assurances that it wouldn't be very cold. She stayed for June and July, and said afterwards that our winter was like an English summer: 'a *good* English summer.' Apart from the cold and the darkness, my strongest memory of London winters is of the sunlight lacking heat: of seeking out sunny patches on the footpath, and never becoming accustomed to the fact that it would be no warmer there.

I've known Judy for twenty-five years. She is my oldest friend, and she came to stay when Luke was fifteen months old. The debate about whether he was, or was not, 'all right' was really getting into its stride by then, and she came to be with me. 'Sometimes,' she said, 'he's as bright as a silver button.'

Her words were an acorn of hope that I kept in my pocket. They sang of nannies and nurseries, of buttered toast and tears before bedtime. They were the last dying note, just about, of the world I was leaving: the world where there would always be someone else to be the grown-up.

8 June

Last Sunday I finished this current phase of planting. I put in a new Virginia creeper and another McCartney rose. These are the Hell's Angels of the suburban garden. I am hoping that they will be the salvation of the narrow patch of ground between the lattice fence and the front footpath. This patch faces west on very exposed ground which we always forget to water. When it is not being ravaged by harsh sunlight, the winter shadow of the Queensland box tree on the verge plunges it into darkness.

I am going to adopt the Italian practice of planting under a waxing moon. The only exception to this rule that I know of is the salad vegetable *radicchio,* which must be planted under a waning moon, *luna cadente;* but I am not planning on starting a vegetable garden. I promised myself when I began that I would concentrate on structure, and not be distracted by the longing for flowers, which is as intense in a Perth garden as it is in London, though for the opposite reason. The bulbs were supposed to satisfy this yearning. Now I find that flowering annuals are on my mind.

The thing is that the arum lilies follow a curve. How pleasing it would be to have a flower garden along that same meander. And the cut flowers would be glorious for the house. In Friday's paper there was a long, luscious list of what you can grow. Hollyhocks, Iceland poppies. *Stock.* I had night-scented stock and hyacinths in window boxes when we lived in London. (Strawberries, too; until the cat caught a baby bird that ventured on to the windowsill to eat them. The bird was so tiny that at first I thought it was a moth.)

But one glance at the gardening book reminds me of what I already know. Annuals, unlike bulbs, do not look after themselves. Weekly applications of soluble fertiliser, no less; and before that, of course, they have to be planted. They are martyrs to insects and mildew. Annuals are serious business.

9 June

The beauty of following the moon's phases is that two weeks each month can be devoted to cleaning up. This is very different from my old approach, which was to plant too many new things, in a rush, and then desert the garden, leaving devastation behind me. So I have two weeks ahead in which to dig and weed, and experience the aches and pains that cleaning up means, before I make any rash decisions about annuals.

Though the early mornings are cold, the days are mostly sunny and mild. The cold returns at about four in the afternoon. Yesterday, though it rained, the sun was shining through the rain for some of the time. Today was exactly the bleak staying indoors sort of day that I have longed for.

I haven't been swimming since the summer. I bought a twelve months' pass at the start of the year to blackmail myself into going regularly again, but it had the opposite effect.

I used to yearn for the water when the children were little and couldn't be left on the beach. (Luke still can't.) The heaving green swells used to call me. I had long, soaking baths instead, in our green bath that's so big you can float in it, and dreamed of being alone.

14 June

It's been nearly a week since I've had a chance to think about this diary, let alone get out into the garden. My work deadlines are more or less met, and the weekend should see me finished, but meanwhile I've let myself be consumed. I'm stiff from sitting locked in one position for interminable stretches of time, and I'm tired. By taking up gardening in a more serious way, I'd hoped to end this pattern. I need another rhythm to live by.

I keep dreaming about folding clothes — children's clothes, freshly washed, with that lovely smell they have, that sunny clean flannel sheet smell, with the smell of the child as well, so that you hold them up to your nose and breathe them in. I dream about sorting men's shirts, too: some of them still in their cellophane wrappers, dusty from neglect.

Now that I have more time I feel terrorised by choice. I can bear to look ahead, as I couldn't when Luke was small; but the future — no longer foreclosed, as it seemed to be then — is far too open for comfort.

15 June

I began the day with high hopes of a weekend in the garden. It was sunny and warm when I was proofreading early this morning. By the time I'd finished, though, the sky had clouded completely over. It's been raining heavily, if intermittently, ever since, and there are occasional loud gusts of wind. A storm has sketched itself out overhead; but so far it has not roused itself to fill in the details. Nevertheless, the adolescent jacaranda trees on the verge are taking it very seriously indeed, and flinging themselves about. In this weather their fronds remind me of the tree branches which point like gloved fingers in *Green Eggs and Ham*.

This always happens, and I am *always* unprepared for it. Having yearned to complete a job, and having jollied myself along with the delightful prospect of two or three weeks' time to myself, I am now at a thoroughly loose end. Maybe my gardening plans have only been a form of subliminal therapy, a carrot in disguise. With time on my hands, ironically, I don't feel like going outside.

The roads are glistening. Patches of brief sunlight turn the day to silver. 'Severe squalls' are in store, according to the news. Last night, the rain was so heavy that the roads were awash, which I don't remember having happened for years.

I rushed my completed text to the bindery first thing yesterday, which was Monday, in order to give myself the week free. Now here I am on Tuesday morning, as gloomy as can be. Luke is home with a bad cold. I've just driven Laurie to the dentist. Mark still has one exam to go, so he's home too; and there's not much incentive to do anything for myself.

20 June

Winter solstice tomorrow. We've had three days of stormy weather: of 'old-fashioned' storms, as I heard them described yesterday. High winds, thunder, lightning, and those torrents of rain I remember from our early years in Perth when it seemed as though the Indian Ocean had simply up-ended and poured itself on to the streets. The paperwhite jonquils which I planted on the verge on Anzac Day have chosen this moment to flower.

I packed Luke off to school today. I was looking forward so much to a day to myself. I was even going to make a start on tidying up the house. Now I've got his sore throat. This fate has been met with a very ill grace. I ventured outside only for a moment, to see whether the foolish jonquils have had their heads blown off yet, but so far they are all right. Not for nothing are they called narcissi.

21 June

Still sick; but it's almost a pleasure, curled up safely in bed, listening to the storm outside.

It is hard, nowadays, to remember a time when I wasn't worried about Luke. We were still in Melbourne when I took him to the local infant health sister for his six weeks' checkup. She commented on how alertly he was looking around; and before I could stop myself I blurted out the words, 'Yes, but he's not smiling yet.' Mark had smiled much earlier. Mark had never stopped gazing, it seemed to me, had never stopped gazing at my face. My new baby did not do this, and neither did he smile.

When I saw the obstetrician a few days later I told him, too, that Luke still wasn't smiling. He was unimpressed. 'It's the younger generation! Haven't you noticed? They're so serious.'

The health centre sister, at least, had paid attention to what I was saying. 'Eight weeks,' she said. 'If he's not smiling by eight weeks, I'd be worried.' But Luke did smile by eight weeks, he smiled right on eight weeks, and all was well again.

24 June

Yesterday afternoon I went outside, when the rain had finally cleared, to see how the jonquils had survived the bad weather. (I'm feeling better.) They've done remarkably well, considering their fragile aspect. They are indeed paper-white: completely so, except for their stamens, which are orange. They are small and — yes — papery in appearance. They look like tiny stars. I counted eight flowers on one stem. The others had five or six. Four plants have flowered so far, and they look quite snug against the wall, but I cut the blooms anyway and brought them inside. (The buds keep on opening indoors.) Their scent is strong for such a dainty flower. It carries with it an intimation of decay, the way jasmine does.

The three roses on the *'Gloire de Dijon'* have

had a far worse time of it. They had not quite opened before the storm hit, and their petals, still loosely wrapped, are brown now, with spots of mould, instead of palest pink. The climbing fig, which serves as scaffolding for this rose, has never fruited before this year. The fruit are a light celadon colour, and hard to see because the leaves camouflage them so effectively; but there must be fifteen or twenty of them. The translucent green is giving way, since the storm, to a thin wash of watery purple.

Meanwhile, the Seville oranges are ripening. Three weeks ago there was nothing to choose between their pale yellow and the lemony green of the weeping mulberry's leaves alongside. Now one wouldn't think to compare them. The mulberry leaves are a strong yellow, edged with brown, and there are far fewer than there were. The oranges are ruddy and bright, but my pleasure in seeing them is mixed. I should be starting to pick them for marmalade about now, because the pectin content is higher when they are not fully ripe.

I have a marvellous recipe — 'Colonel Gore's' — which suits me very well, because it is made over a three-day period.

You do a bit to the mixture each day, which cuts out the day-long haul of normal jam making; and the final cooking only takes an hour and a half. Why, then, am I not looking forward to it?

25 June

We planted two orange trees a year or so after we moved to this house. We came here in the winter, in late July or early August (I can never remember exactly when because the house was vacant and we were allowed to move in a little ahead of the settlement date). The first few months were a time of constant surprises, as the garden slowly opened itself to us, with the coming of spring. Trees which we had thought were dead began putting out green shoots. The robinia and two of the pomegranates revealed themselves. Then there was a citrus tree, overgrown and scrawny, which we took to be an old cumquat gone to wood. It turned out to be an Imperial mandarin, which yielded a good twenty kilos of fruit the following year.

We decided that our garden might be a good place to try more citrus trees. At the nursery, we chose the only two we recognised: a Washington navel, for eating, and a Seville. Apart from the beauty of the Seville's name, and its long, exotic history, I was attracted by the idea of making marmalade with the traditional fruit, grown in our own garden.

There was no shortage of time in those days. What was lacking was a sense of accomplishment. Caring for babies and toddlers requires undemanding, friendly tasks which can be put aside easily. Apart from the endless rounds of nappies and meals, nothing else ever seems to get done. The children are kept clean, and fed, and, if you're lucky, safe; and that's it. As Virginia Woolf said, 'All the dinners are cooked; the plates and cups washed; the children sent to school and gone out into the world. Nothing remains of it all.'

So the orange trees were planted, and later transplanted, which slowed down their growth; and the years went by. About seven years ago they began to fruit in a regular, serious-minded sort of a way.

That's when my problems started. The Washington navel is overshadowed by the

Japanese pepper tree, and does not get enough sunlight to fruit well, but the Seville is always laden. Even in an off year it has about fifty oranges, and in a good year, easily three times that. Had I planted it for ornamental purposes I would presumably be able to enjoy the glorious spectacle of it, unencumbered by feelings of guilt. Each year I would remind myself of the orange groves on the Palatine Hill in Rome, in the Farnese Gardens, and the fruit left hanging there till it falls, and I would reflect on the pleasure our orange tree must give to passers-by, where it hangs over the north-facing wall.

But I did not plant it to look pretty. I planted it for marmalade. This year has been an especially good one. The oranges are a little on the small side: because of the dry summer, I suppose, but there are masses and masses of them. I cannot look at them without dwelling on the marmalade which I ought to be making.

2 July

There is to be another full moon at the end of July, on the thirtieth, so that my birthday will be bracketed by two full moons in one month! I read yesterday that the second is called a blue moon. They are not as rare as one might imagine from the expression they have given rise to. Blue moons can occur within a month or so of each other, and are never more than two years and four months apart.

The sky was clear this morning. Then the wind blew up again. Now there is a covering of silver and grey cloud, quite low, that's getting denser by the minute.

The paperwhite jonquils are almost all in flower. Their strong scent is perfuming the verge. Even with my cold, I can smell them. The biggest of the crabapples, which flowered unexpectedly for a second time in May, is now completely bare. The two roses in pots on the brick walk are in bud. (Is this my fault? They were looking brown and lanky at the end of May, so I pruned them early. I enjoy pruning, and go to it with a will, but this doesn't mean that I know how to do it.)

I gave them some rose food, because they looked so sorry for themselves. Now the apricot bush rose, 'Just Joey', has three buds, and the floribunda, 'Friesia', which is yellow, has one. Despite the cold, there are aphids in evidence. They must have tougher constitutions than I do.

The weeping mulberry has some leaves left, near its crown, but the branches of the Virginia creeper are quite bare. They have an etiolated yet sculpted appearance, their convolutions full of character. You'd think, though, that they were dead.

3 July

I'm somewhat out of sorts. I was all set to tidy the house completely, clean out my office, even do my tax. Instead I'm sick. Simply keeping up to date with the washing is an achievement under these circumstances.

Picture this. A home movie, a brief snatch of Super 8; glaring, low-angled sunlight. Perth in the winter. A young woman seated on the lawn with her two babies. One a little boy, chubby-faced, talking, moving a lot. He's about three, maybe three and a half. Not four. The other a stolid, squat baby-in-arms, knitted hat, woolly cardigan.

He's not looking anywhere in particular; his mother, who's propping him up, is smiling at the camera.

Look again. It's another sunny, cold day: the same day, it looks like, because the children don't seem any older, but then you become aware that they've got different clothes on and are seated in a slightly different spot. Still, if you weren't looking closely, you'd assume it was a continuation of the earlier scene; and you wouldn't pay much attention anyway, would you? Film like this, the high colour, the slightly slowed down movement, the glowing faces: there must be miles and miles of it in suburban Australian homes.

Then you notice their expressions. The triangle of faces has been soldered into a single travelling gaze. The three-year-old is staring up at his mother, his face stricken. Her eyes are fixed on the baby.

I'm feeling angry as I write this. It was too hard to live through then; and it's too hard to write about now. The lounge room floor is strewn with photographs. Luke loves looking at them, especially the pictures of his childhood, but he never tidies up afterwards;

and I have to be in the right frame of mind to do it. The albums were up to date in time for Luke's birth; they haven't been touched since. We have boxes of loose photographs, instead.

Loose photographs you can shuffle about. You can pick them up and put them down again in any order you like. Photo albums are for happy families. Children, grown-up, pass them on to their children. When you are thirty-one years old, and the soaring curve of your carefully planned future suddenly freezes into stillness against the sky, photo albums are the first thing to go.

I don't remember the home movie being taken. We had Laurie's father's Super 8 reels transferred on to video a few years ago, as a present for him; when I was watching the copy we kept for ourselves I found those scraps at the very end of the tape. We'd brought the movie camera back with us to Perth after Luke was born, to keep a record of the babies' growth for our parents in Melbourne. That's how it must have happened.

4 July

This cold is a particularly persistent one. Moira at the video shop says it lasted eight weeks with her, and one of Mark's friends' mothers had it for four. There are days where you feel better, and think that it's over, and days when you know it's back again. There are days when you simply feel tired.

Heavy rain today, interspersed with promising (deceptive?) periods of bright sunshine.

5 July

Another jonquil has flowered on the verge! It has creamy white outside petals, and what appears to be a double centre, which is buttery yellow. I planted four grand monarch jonquils out there, and it may be one of them, though it isn't much like the illustration on the packet. Otherwise, it will be a cuckoo in the paperwhite nest. It has an extraordinary scent, like a lemony jasmine. I must make an effort to identify it promptly, in case it's the only one and I end up searching fruitlessly for others in future years.

Something is feasting on the petals of one of the paperwhites. I'm tempted to go on another picking spree, and enjoy them, while they last, in the house, instead of leaving them to the predators outside.

The winter jasmine is studded, suddenly, with yellow flowers.

6 July

I pruned the winter jasmine back hard in May. It had been shading the Spanish broom which we put in more than a year ago, and which has so far failed to flower. The jasmine was also keeping the sun from the bed where I've planted about thirty pheasant's eye daffodils. (They may still not be getting enough sun. There is no sign of them at all yet, whereas others of the same variety, which I planted in pots on the brick walk, are starting to come up.)

Shopping at dusk the other evening, I was carrying heavy bags through the supermarket car park when all at once I was in London again. It's more than twenty years since we lived there, but the cold, the misty clouds around the street lights, and the exhaust smells of the traffic going past on the highway had taken me abruptly back. We lived there for four years, studying, when we were first married.

Mostly, in our conversations about the past, Laurie and I look back on this as a golden age; that halcyon time, away from home at last, when we were alone as a couple together, before the children came. This time, though, I remembered the bleakness of those endless winters, trudging home from the supermarket, in the cold and dark, to an empty house.

A fine, sunny day; the first, as it seems, for weeks.

7 July

Giving way to being ill has left me in limbo. I can't even occupy myself by worrying about the commercial work that's not getting done — normally a fruitful source of tension — because it's all up to date.

No one knew what might be the matter with our bright-eyed boy. All we could do was wait, and see, and meanwhile play with him. Hour after hour, day after day, I'd sing and chant. Having no words, he nevertheless liked tunes, and they became the leitmotifs that structured his existence. We'd take him back to the specialist, proud of what he had learned; but always there was a new loss to be faced; a new skill, overdue for his age, which had failed to appear.

We never got used to the shock of it. Back at the house it would be Laurie who hung the nappies out to dry, Laurie who began to chop the vegetables for dinner. Laurie who built a fortress around all of us, while I held my baby and wept.

Laurie was far more worried about me than he was about Luke. In those early days, neither he nor anyone else in our families could understand what was wrong — not with Luke, but with me. Why court trouble? our parents wondered aloud. I was overwrought, in everyone's eyes; the doctors were alarmists.

'Even the doctors weren't definite,' says Laurie, looking back. '"Delay" was the word they used, which surely meant that Luke would catch up. Certainly he was different from Mark, but it wasn't fair to compare them. Mark was like quicksilver. It was asking too much to expect another Mark.'

Luke was nearly three before Laurie could begin to bear to doubt. By then I had a student in to help me in the summer holidays, the first of a succession of babysitters; and Laurie caught her looking at Luke one time, when she thought no one was watching. 'Her expression was ... quizzical, somehow. And *sad*.' And he thought to himself, '*Oh*. It's not only Carolyn.'

16 July

'Rain and gales,' as the paper puts it. When the winds are fierce, the rain can drive against you like nails. George Seddon was right. Perth is not so much poised on the southwestern edge of the Australian continent as perched on the easternmost shore of the Indian Ocean. Our weather comes from there.

I have to admit I'm disappointed in the garden. I have been sustaining myself with a vision of perfection which will be impossible to achieve. All I can see is the long bank of sand on the verge.

Far from flowering, some of the bulbs in pots seem to have rotted, and lots haven't come up. Worst of all, my mother-in-law explained to me on the phone that too much fertiliser, with both orchids and lilies, encourages them to put on lots of leafy growth — but that's all. It will be at least a year, she thinks, before I see my arum lilies return.

It's depressing; and yet nothing has changed except my perception of it. Most depressing of all is the fact that I don't even *like* immaculate gardens! What must I have been thinking of?

17 July

Last night I woke in a terrible fright. I did not know which bed I was in, nor which house. Worst of all was the conviction that the children were not there: that somehow we had lost them.

Driving to Cottesloe yesterday, I was aware, as never before, of how gaunt Perth's trees are. The expectation of resistance is built into them. They always appear to be fighting an invisible force. The gale-strength winds of the last few nights are a demonstration of what they have steeled themselves against, over the years. But our pink dog rose has one fresh bloom on it, and seeing it made me feel better. It is a deep pink colour, which one seldom sees on these roses in the summer, because the sun makes them fade so quickly. It's not a dog rose at all, in fact, but a modern variety, a climber called 'Sparrieshoop'; the open single petals and the prominent stamens give it that effect.

There's soft rain falling, as I write this. The winds are at rest today, but two branches of our cocos palm are down.

19 July

How deaf Missy is now. It's happened so fast that it makes me wonder whether it may not be old age at all but something curable. I've been putting off taking her to the vet because she's so smelly. She's a yard dog, and so we don't notice it, but in an enclosed space the vet certainly will. It's too cold to give her a bath.

Sebastian has never forgiven us for taking Missy in. He has conveniently forgotten that he was taken in, too. He used to belong to Melinda, our neighbour Diana's daughter. It has been war to the death ever since Missy celebrated her arrival by chasing Sebastian up the Japanese pepper tree. Missy lived in the house across the street. She must have spent years watching Sebastian, and biding her time. When she finally came to us she took instant possession of the garden, and Sebastian was forced to retreat to the house. Now that Missy is deaf, and not seeing too well either, Sebastian — who can't be much younger, but whose faculties are somewhat more intact — is bent on reclaiming the night.

20 July

Although it was still cloudy last night, the new moon was occasionally visible: a thin saucer of gold, cupping a fine outline of what will be the full moon's shape. This sliver is the beginning of the blue moon.

The jonquils have finished but there is no sign of any other bulb flowering, except for the single white hyacinth which I planted in a blue and yellow ceramic pot. The perfume is already detectable. I am assuming that everything else in the pots must be waterlogged. As for the bulbs in the ground which haven't sprouted, they must be in too shady a position. The garden is grey and silent. The brick walk has large patches of slippery green moss: an unusual sight in Perth. Still, I'm depressed about the bulbs. I know I took them on as an experiment, but it was easy to be optimistic in the heady, warm days of autumn. It's harder now. What if even those that have sprouted don't flower?

The only signs of life, apart from the hyacinth, are small green shoots on two of our shrubs. They produce scented blue flowers fading to white, in summer I think, so that you have blue and white flowers together on the bush. They have been looking very straggly and bare, so that I was afraid the summer might have damaged them. The new shoots are a comfort.

It's Saturday, and I'm off to a workshop on dream interpretation for the day. I've been keeping a record of my dreams for some time, but making sense of them is difficult on your own. There's a Jungian analyst from America here at the moment. I'm hoping for some guidelines from her workshop.

23 July

Strong winds again this evening. It sounds as though there's another wild night in store.

I brought the hyacinth indoors late today. It's now on the kitchen windowsill, perfuming the air for me as I work at the sink. When I went out to get it, I noticed that the buds on the Just Joey rose never opened. They are brown and decaying, victims of my premature pruning. The rose bushes along the central beds on Kings Park Road have only just been done, I saw this morning. Sometimes I think that the garden does much better when I leave it alone.

The weeping mulberry has no leaves left at all. At first, it seemed as though there were knots of brown leaves still, wrapped closely about its crown, but they are actually the natural thickening of its uppermost branches.

It is at last becoming more of a grown-up tree. The jacarandas on the verge are still behaving like teenagers; and I'd given up hoping that the weeping mulberry would ever look any different from the half-grown lion cub it so closely resembled when we planted it: gangling, poised for flight. Now it is developing the aspect of an adult tree, albeit a young adult. It was five years old when we planted it, I think, so it must be getting on for seventeen now. Luke's age.

The noise of the galahs at around four every afternoon is becoming routine. They are my favourite bird, both for personality and for plumage. I never hear them without my heart lifting. There has been a colony of about twenty or thirty down on the river foreshore for years, but that is some distance from here. At the cemetery, which is only a few streets away, there is a separate family of five, whose numbers have recently increased to seven. Seeing them has long been one of the highlights of my walks through the cemetery with Missy, but I never expected to have galahs any closer to our house than that.

The foreshore group must have reached its maximum size to be planning an outpost up this way. Much as one might hope for friendly relations to be established between the two tribes, this is not the direction in which matters are heading. Instead, there is a battle royal going on; and, judging by the proximity of the sounds, it is taking place in the trees round our house. I would so love to set up a feeder — thus establishing a further *casus belli* in my own right, I suppose — but the experts on wild birds are absolutely clear in their advice that one must not do it, as the birds become dependent on the food left out; and I have to admit that the droppings would drive me mad.

Tomorrow, my friend Sue is taking me to the zoo for my birthday treat from her. I was allowed to choose anything I wanted. I haven't yet seen the savannah park, which has been open for more than a year. I hope the weather is all right. I don't mind it blustery, but I draw the line at drenching rain.

Off to bed. It's pouring with rain outside. Debris has blocked the gutters again, and at the overflow points water is cascading down from the roof.

Off to bed.

25 July

When I became forty, and then forty-one, and forty-two, a change of pace slowly forced itself upon me. It happened despite my best intentions. I'd catapulted myself back to work years before. Looking for contracts, trying for grants. But once I reached my forties, haste ceased to be attractive. Household chores which had previously been rushed through, or sold off, or ignored altogether, began to sing to me.

It was now, by happy coincidence, that the Seville orange tree started to produce an annual crop; and so, of all the domestic tasks which had unexpectedly begun to chorus their siren songs, it was marmalade which sang loudest. Even the search for a suitable recipe, old enough to specify Seville oranges, became an adventure, pleasurable in its slowness. The painstaking process of getting accustomed to the recipe, and to the oranges, could not be hurried. When, with my third batch, I finally found the right setting point for the jam, my satisfaction was boundless.

The secret lies in the pectin. Despite what the cookery writers say, the pips in Seville oranges, satisfyingly robust though they are, do not contain enough pectin to set the jam by themselves. You can supplement them with shop-bought pectin, but the texture will suffer. The thing to do is to collect extra pips beforehand — from apples, from other oranges — and add them to the muslin bag that goes in the boiling pan. The marmalade should set in twenty minutes.

That first year, I gave it all away in containers begged from friends. The second year, I bought special jars, and kept it for Christmas presents. It was in the following year, I guess, that it began to be a chore. I insisted on using all the oranges on the tree, making batch after batch; and I wanted the jars to be of a certain size and quality. Then I decided that, as presents, they needed raffia at the neck of the jar and a trimming of gum nuts. The next year, needless to say, I didn't make any marmalade.

The weather is still stormy. I haven't gone into the garden except to rescue more jonquils. Nothing else has flowered. The arum lilies, in particular, are a worry.

They've put on lots of leaves, and are much bigger than usual, but there's not a flower stalk to be seen. Laurie is siding with his mother. 'All the gardening books agree that if a plant is doing well you should leave it alone.' (He is much closer to being a serious gardener than I am, though on more of a theoretical basis.)

27 July

The squalls began again early this morning. The winds are very high and there are sudden bursts of lashing rain. A dead fin whale has been washed up on the beach at Cottesloe. It is estimated to weigh forty tonnes or more, and it is twenty metres long: as big as a bus, someone said. Fin whales are the second biggest species of whale. They live all over the world, but only in deep water. Since they do not swim near land, this particular whale is not likely to have been a casualty of the stormy weather. It is thought to have been dead for about a week and driven inshore by the storms.

The winds are certainly howling. Three times now I have heard an odd groaning noise, which makes me fearful that one of our trees is about to fall. Every few minutes I hear the wailing sound of sirens in the distance: whether police cars or ambulances, I can't tell. There is a road weather alert, as there has been so often over the past month.

Luke had planned to be dropped in Claremont to choose his weekend videos and have lunch at Hungry Jack's before making his own way home on the bus. It is his newest, most independent treat, but the weather makes it too risky today. He's very obliging by nature and hasn't made a fuss. Instead, I'll wait for him at Video City and bring him back by car. He's at his Saturday morning drama class, so I still have some time to myself.

What annoys me is that yesterday was fine, and I spent it shut up indoors, working at the Battye Library, and planning the weekend's gardening.

28 July

A sunny Sunday morning. Laurie's cleaning out the gutters and I've just put a load of washing on the line. It's the first time in a month that I haven't had to bundle it all in the car and take it to the laundrette to be dried. I want to plant my geranium cuttings before the full moon on Tuesday. I'm scared that they may be washed away as soon as the weather turns bad again; but they have been growing sturdily in a bowl of water on the kitchen windowsill for the last two months, so they must be pretty tough. They are left over from my pruning bout in May.

I dreamed again last night of missing children. This time it was Luke, newborn in my dream. I'd left him in the care of the nursing staff for three days so that I could have a rest before taking him home from hospital. I was frightened he wouldn't know me after so long, and I was searching for him. It took a while, when I woke, to remind myself that he was spending the night at Trevor's place, and that Mark was safely asleep in bed.

On Friday at the Battye I started late, having been lured over to the art gallery by the Annie Leibovitz exhibition, and then distracting myself further by a visit to CraftWest to buy a brooch for Laurie's sister for Christmas. All this meant that I worked through lunchtime, and well into the afternoon, which I usually do not do; and I was plagued by dragging doubt that someone might be needing me, that I should call home. I was reading the most fascinating material about working lives in the Cottesloe area; but all through it part of my mind kept figuring out, over and over again, where the nearest phone was.

29 July

So far, the hyacinth is the one bulb I've planted which has turned out to be exactly as I'd imagined. I brought it inside when it had only just begun to flower, because I thought enjoying it as it was would be preferable to having it reduced to tatters by the weather. In fact, it has kept on opening. As good as a batch of marmalade, and a lot less work.

31 July

Perhaps I'm being too despondent about my lack of success with the bulbs. It's just that, in my mind's eye, my image of how they would be was completely different from the way they actually are. I guess I underestimated them. I thought that, whatever it said on the packet about different varieties flowering at different times, this would not actually be the case. Not for me. (Certainly not in Perth, where climate variations are far from subtle.) I didn't allow for the possibility that bulbs might have minds of their own. My vision of the perfect garden had everything flowering at the same time, and this is hard to relinquish.

In any case, I may be jumping to conclusions. We've had three or four days in a row where there have been substantial periods of sunshine in between the squalls. Not only have I managed to dry two loads of washing *on the line*, but I've also noticed three or four green shoots in bulb pots which previously showed no sign of life. A solitary grand monarch jonquil has appeared, as well.

Bulbs of the same variety, planted together, don't flower in unison. I knew this, of course, about other things. Children especially. But having it played out in my own garden is an object lesson. Paperwhite jonquils, for instance, turn out to be very independently minded. And there is no sign at all of flowers from any of the other grand monarch jonquils, apart from that one.

1 August

Every bud on the hyacinth has come out now. It is fresh and white and perfect. The pomegranate tree outside the kitchen has new red leaves sprouting all along its branches.

I keep opening the fridge and staring vacantly in. Time to cook dinner. Laurie does most of the cooking nowadays but tonight it's my turn. Chicken and mushroom pie. It means making stock — perfunctory as my cooking is these days, I draw the line at pre-packed stock — and preparing a velouté sauce. It's a way of keeping these skills from atrophying completely, but the puff pastry is from the supermarket, so the assembly part is easy. Sue (who also went to cooking classes in her youth) has sunk even further than I. She confessed to me the other day that she uses a barbecued chicken, and bacon instead of sautéed mushrooms. I was shocked.

3 August

I've cleaned the kitchen windows. The

difference it makes! The long shafts of sunlight from the north can now slip under the eaves and into the room. Lying on the kitchen sofa and gazing out is a new experience.

I've also waxed the furniture, especially the big nursery table, which smells of camphor now. I still haven't made any marmalade, though, and the oranges are beginning to fall.

5 August

I'm pleased I spent the whole of Sunday in the garden. Today is overcast. The clouds are a deep, forbidding bluish-grey. I can hear the constant drip of the downpipes on to the bricks, in between the heavy falls of rain which drown out every other sound but their own.

Yesterday, it was sunny both morning and afternoon. The first properly fine day in ages. There were two periods when the sky grew dark, and the temperature dropped abruptly; so much so that I was convinced I would have to give up, and go indoors. But the rain did not come. I weeded the brick walk. I hadn't wanted to disturb the moss, which is such a pleasing sight between the old orange bricks, but the weeds have been taking advantage.

The rest of the time it was a matter of cleaning up and raking leaves. Normally, I like to let the leaves lie, particularly under the big front tree, but they are soaking wet and mouldy now: no longer the pale yellow carpet that they were in autumn. I was also concerned that they might stop the dichondra from spreading. I have great hopes of it, and of the limestone court. What's really doing well is the double white violet, The Czar, as it's called. (I was misled by the Latin name, *Viola odorata*, into mistaking it for a viola.) It's spreading with a recklessness which only the summer sun will curb.

I also cut the dead flowers off the Bird of Paradise and had a go at trimming the purple lantana underneath it. I remember lantanas from my childhood in Brisbane. There was a speckled pink and yellow one there (I've also seen it here in Perth), which was similar in colour to my favourite freckled variety of conversation lolly; so much so that I always imagine for an instant, on seeing one, that it has the same delicious musk smell, instead of that highly pungent odour.

My preferred mode of gardening in winter used to be to go to the nursery on a sunny day and buy attractive plants in flower, so that I would have a fresh, colourful show. I was philosophical about the fact that few of them lasted for long. Survival wasn't the point. It felt strange yesterday not to be doing this; and it feels strange today to look out at a garden which is barer (if a little tidier), for all my efforts, than it was before.

(I didn't entirely succeed in resisting the trip to the nursery. I did go, to buy eight packets of nasturtium seeds.)

There are tiny white buds on the Washington navel, and the polyanthus jasmine on top of the wall has slender, deep pink fingertips.

9 August

A neighbour, who introduced himself as Jim, has come round asking if he can take the Seville oranges off my hands! He makes marmalade for St Vincent de Paul, and raised nearly two thousand dollars last year. This year he's made six hundred jars; and he's got his eye on our tree.

In one way, it solves my problem, so I was surprised at myself when I didn't immediately agree. If I'm not using the oranges myself, I realise, I want the spectacle of them, hanging there. ('The Palatine syndrome', Laurie calls it. Gracious living in ancient Rome.)

What will probably swing the balance is the fact that Jim has offered to do a trade: a jar of his apple, lemon and lime special blend in return. He says you can either have it on toast for breakfast or use it to baste a roast. (You put the jam on the meat about five minutes before you're due to take it out of the oven.)

Our wedding anniversary turned out better than I expected. I cooked lamb stuffed with apricots and prunes, my favourite dish, and trifle, which is Laurie's. Then we went to Luke's school play. Mark came too. This is the third occasion the four of us have gone out together recently.

11 August

I spent today weeding in the garden. I felt the activity expand to fill my mind. The weeding became an end in itself. Instead of rushing ahead in my thoughts, to a time when it would all be done, I slowed my pace, and simply sat on the ground (on a plastic cushion), and weeded. Winter must be made for weeding. The ground is soft and wet, so that the weeds come up easily. The sun is not too hot on your back. While I was driving up to Landsdale to collect Luke from camp, though, my muscles must have stiffened, because when I got out of the car I couldn't stand up properly.

Apparently he had a good time. A production of *Grease* at Girrawheen Senior High School yesterday evening, according to the information sheet that came home with him, and a football match today. ('What did you like best, Luke?' 'Choosing videos.')

I've been reading the letters of the poet Philip Larkin. ('They fuck you up, your mum and dad ...') In one, written in December 1974, he says, 'Have been wreaking a special kind of havoc known as "pruning the roses".' This has made me feel better about my own efforts. Also, though I do not mean to boast, the yellow freesia has two beautifully shaped flowers on it, and the buds on the Just Joey, which I despaired of, did eventually bloom into three enormous roses, two of which are in the vase next to me as I write. They are wonderfully fragrant. (Laurie says they are not meant to be cabbage roses, and that I am never to use rose fertiliser again, but I am thrilled with them. I love cabbage roses.)

Now for the bulb bulletin. Three of the grand monarch jonquils which I planted alongside the paperwhites are in flower, together with a single yellow daffodil. In a pot next to the front step, two 'Erlicheer' daffodils are about to come out. They have multiple heads of tiny double flowers, so that you would take them for jonquils. From what I can see so far, they are a rich cream in colour. They are supposed to have a marvellous scent, and I can't wait to smell them.

The white hyacinth has produced a second flower! It is a most satisfactory plant. I've put it outside again where it can have the benefit of the sun.

12 August

There are two clusters of open flowers among the branches of the polyanthus jasmine. I'd always found its nutty perfume intoxicating, without ever understanding why, until I went back to Brisbane, to the house where my family lived from the time I was three until I was six, and smelled — from streets away — the smell of my childhood. It was the pink flowering shrub outside the fence of the house next door.

Someone has said that going back to a childhood place is like stepping into a fairytale. Returning to Kedron after thirty-five years, I couldn't believe that the same people weren't still living there. (I couldn't believe that *I* wasn't still there.) A neighbour who came out to check on me said she knew of no one from so long ago. The one constant was the shrub next door. I took armfuls of it back with me to my hotel, somewhat to the disdain of the desk staff. Perhaps it's all too common in the suburbs of Brisbane.

I pressed a flower to bring back to Perth so that Laurie could identify it. *Luculia gratissima*, it turned out to be. It's not an indigenous plant: it comes from the

Himalayas. We planted two when we'd found out what it was, but they both died within a year. 'For no apparent reason they will often die, even when some years old,' says Walter G Hazlewood in his *Handbook of Trees, Shrubs and Roses*. 'It is very temperamental and causes more heartbreak than any other shrub.' In its absence, the pink-tinged jasmine does duty for the luculia of long ago.

14 August

It was Laurie's idea to concentrate on scented species. We decided against an indigenous garden when we moved to this house, even though, in 1980, they were very popular, and said to be the answer to the dry summers of Perth. We wanted as much deep green foliage as we could muster, for our personal antidote to the heat. Wherever we could, we've chosen perfumed varieties.

We had no idea then how hard it would be to establish an exotic garden, or what it would cost to water it. The two luculias were not the only plants to cause us heartbreak. The big trees, however — the robinia and the Japanese pepper — were already old when we came here, and they helped a lot because of the filtered light they provided to young plants.

Of all the scented plants we've tried, the jasmines have been the best.

18 August

How to describe the weather now that spring is less than two weeks away? In the first place, it has been much colder this last week: near freezing point before sunrise, and very cold at night. Setting off in the morning at eight to drive Luke to school (because Laurie, who normally does it, has an early start this week), I've been wearing gloves and a hat. The road and the trees are grey and misty at that hour, though the sun is already shining. I love the sensation of living in a cold climate.

The days, though, are sparkling and clear, and the sky an intense Mediterranean blue. I've seen people in the early afternoons wearing shirts and shorts because that part of the day is so warm. This bright sunlight is the second change. The third is that the rain has organised itself into set periods.

There is also the undeniable fact that spring flowers are appearing: and not just bulbs, which, after all, are easily deceived by Perth's mild climate. Apart from the polyanthus jasmine, the iceberg climbing roses are also putting on a fine display. I cannot make much of this, because they flower for most of the year, but it can nevertheless be said that, where there were none a month ago, there are now more than two dozen.

A better guide, perhaps, is the first McCartney rose, which is rearing up from the shrubbery overhanging the sunny side of the wall. This rose flowers for only a month each year, in early spring, but the sight of that shining circle of enamelled white petals, set off by bright yellow stamens in the centre, is worth the eleven months' wait. Even the long, deep scratches on hands and arms are worth it.

The white hyacinth is back on the kitchen windowsill. The second bloom is almost as big and as sweetly scented as the first. So far, it has been the bulb which has provided the greatest reward for the least trouble. There is a second Erlicheer flower indoors. Its buttery colour comes from the fact that between every two rows of cream, mitre-shaped petals, there is a quite different layer of rounded, semi-transparent yellow ones. From the scent particularly, I would say that the cuckoo which flowered among the paperwhite jonquils a month ago must have been one of these.

The question remains whether it is a daffodil or a jonquil. Even though the bulbs came in a packet of mixed scented daffodils, there is a pot of them — very expensive! — on sale in Claremont as jonquils. I've checked in the dictionary, and all it says is that both are varieties of *Narcissus*, though the implication is that daffodils have a single trumpet flower and jonquils, a multiple head (in which case the Erlicheer can safely be called a jonquil).

19 August

It is a feature of these clear, sunny days, after cold nights, that they are absolutely cloudless.

There is a wild freesia in flower on the verge. Our garden used to be thick with them, but after we built the wall they died out almost entirely. Laurie has found a second McCartney rose in flower, this time on the crabapple side of the wall. The bush is laden with buds; in about a week the flowers will be too numerous to count.

I've been pressing ahead with the weeding. I'm keen to plant the nasturtiums I bought, but I'm making myself wait until the weeding is finished. The Virginia creeper I planted on the westernmost edge of the garden has new leaves on it. It's heading away from the wall as fast as it can, in search of sunlight. I'm very much afraid it's not going to find any. Since I've been paying more attention, I've noticed that the sun doesn't reach that patch until well into the afternoon, by which time it's shaded not only by the Queensland box tree on the verge in front of it but also by another on the opposite side of the street. I doubt this will alter substantially in summer.

The new McCartney rose has lost nearly all its leaves. (Too much fertiliser.) There are two furled, white-tipped stalks in the arum lily bed, however, so all may not be lost in that quarter.

The big Virginia creeper round the side of

the house is still completely bare.

Last week we transplanted the West Indian lime, which was near the kitchen window, to a new position on the other side of the wall next to the lavender bushes where there is more sun. (The frangipani died.) It looks happier already. It hadn't grown at all in the three years since it was put in. I hope it improves now, though I suppose it's too late to expect any blossom, and hence any fruit next winter.

The mandarins are like small round bullets. Most of them fell off early because they didn't get enough water in the summer, and the ground is carpeted with them. The tree looks a bit like the cumquat we originally thought it was.

25 August

Our third day of sunshine, after a period of several rainy days. There's a definite breath of spring in the air today: that warm, balmy sensation, uplifting to the spirits. The smell that sent Mole off on his adventures.

I've weakened. I've brought enough pink

and white garlands of jasmine inside to fill a vase. I shouldn't let myself be tempted into cutting them, because they only last a day or two, and they are heartstoppingly beautiful on the vine. But the perfume is filling the house.

The moon is waxing fast. All I've succeeded in planting thus far is a single packet of nasturtium seeds. What I want is a dibble. Lacking one, I've used the thin end of the small blue kitchen funnel, with predictable results. (The seeds are safely in the ground, but the funnel has vanished.)

I'm keen to put in some more violets. The Czar violets are spreading with such youthful energy that I feel I can safely transplant some of the clumps. Violets have been a bit of a sadness this year. The Parma violets in the front garden were completely extinguished by the heat, even though they were never in direct sunlight. They'd done so well, for so many years, that I'd begun to take them for granted, and paid them no attention in the very summer that they needed it most. They'd probably have survived with extra watering.

The colony under the mandarin tree did a little better. Several plants lived, and they've just lately been flowering. This last week, a bunch of Parma violets, with two of the white doubles as well, has been gracing the miniature blue and white jug.

27 August

A surprise when I went outside! I can see blue petals emerging from what I now realise is the calyx of an iris. I'd given up all hope of the irises. I planted two pots of them, supposedly mixed yellow and blue, some of a variety called 'Professor Blaauw'. Until today, there had been nothing to show for these efforts but long, strappy, rather tired leaves. I'd convinced myself they weren't going to flower. In fact, I'd gone out this morning, mug of tea in hand, with the express purpose of a mournful walk along the brick path to reflect on my wasted labours. There was not a single bulb in bloom yesterday.

This, I must confess, is partly because I cut what few there were the day before, on the excuse that heavy rain was forecast. They are in a jug in the kitchen: two yellow trumpet daffodils, two Erlicheers, and two grand monarch jonquils. The grand monarch is the jonquil you generally see in florists' shops. It has a yellow centre, with a single row of white petals. It is large, with a stalk as thick as a daffodil's, and a strong scent. Striking as it is, and easy as it must be to grow, it has not the delicate appearance or the subtle perfume of the paperwhite or the Erlicheer varieties. (That's assuming the Erlicheer to be a jonquil. I haven't found it — under either denomination — in any of the books I've looked at so far.)

I am foolish to let my vision of masses of nodding heads get in the way of the extreme pleasure these bulbs are giving me. You'd think the six gleaming blooms on the window ledge were newly minted, so fresh and clean are they. Their perfume was the first thing I noticed when I woke up this morning. It is so strong that it reaches past the kitchen to our bedroom beyond.

When Wordsworth went on the expedition which resulted in his poem 'Daffodils', he was accompanied by his sister, Dorothy. It was she, in fact, who wrote the first description of what they saw.

When we were in the woods beyond Gowbarrow park we saw a few daffodils close to the water-side. We fancied that the lake had floated the seeds ashore, and that the little colony had so sprung up. But as we went along there were more and yet more and at last under the boughs of the trees, we saw that there was a long belt of them along the shore, about the breadth of a country turnpike road. I never saw daffodils so beautiful they grew among the mossy stones about and about them, some rested their heads upon these stones as on a pillow for weariness and the rest tossed and reeled and danced and seemed as if they verily laughed with the wind that blew upon them over the lake, they looked so gay ever glancing ever changing. This wind blew directly over the lake to them. There was here and there a little knot and a few stragglers a few yards higher up but they were so few as not to disturb the simplicity and unity and life of that one busy highway.

It is this word picture, or rather the picture as redrawn by her brother, which stands like a screen in front of my mind's eye and prevents me from seeing my daffodils as they are.

Last night, I dreamed Luke was driving me in the car. He's often in my dreams. It used to be that I would be late picking him up, and frantic about him waiting for me in the dark. Last night, though, I was worried about him driving, and he was reassuring me — 'I've done this road *twice*!' — like any teenager.

28 August

In your mind, when you're pregnant, you carry a fantasy child. You don't notice you're doing it. You don't notice that it's a fantasy, either. In your mind it's the child that will be.

Usually, with the arrival of the actual baby, it is so intensely itself, right from the very instant of its birth, that the fantasy child at once takes flight, and vanishes forever, being only the palest shadow of the reality. But when the baby comes, and somehow, almost immediately, you don't know quite how, you're worried that something may be wrong, then the fantasy child doesn't leave. It hangs about, and haunts you.

Old-fashioned stories of changelings are thought to have evolved to explain the presence in a household of an otherworldly child, a child who failed to respond. (Such a child, say, as might be diagnosed with autism, now.) Sometimes I felt that we, too, had fallen under an enchantment.

I would watch Luke, between two and three years of age, in the abandonment of sleep. I would drink him in, in the stillness. By day, he was boisterous and difficult. In his cot, long-limbed, asleep, he was perfection. Exhausted as I was from looking after him, I would gaze at the olive-skinned legs flung out on the white sheet, and I would *know*, beyond all doubt, that nothing could be wrong with such a beautiful child.

Hoping against hope, I went on too long reassuring Laurie, when he begged me to, that Luke would be all right. In the end, sitting by the fire one winter's night, I finally had to tell him I couldn't do that any more — not even for his sake. It was the worst night of my life.

29 August

Luke's been home sick for days. He's got an infected throat and it's apparently very sore. For me, though, it's meant no break since his mid-term holiday, because he became ill straight afterwards. (Not, needless to say, during.) The energy I put into planning outings during his four days' holiday has more than dissipated, as has my resolutely cheerful mien.

The blue iris has flowered, to take me out of myself. Standing on the brick walk, lost in admiration, I noticed the scent of the michelia, some distance away. The *Michelia* species are named after Pier Antonio Micheli, a Florentine botanist, who died in 1737. Ours is *Michelia figo*, so called because the leaves have some resemblance to those of a small fig tree. The flowers are mainly white, with a port-wine tint, and unobtrusive, but their perfume is sweetish peppermint. You can't detect it up close. It's strongest about two metres from the plant. Why? What does it want to attract that needs luring from further away?

Part Three
Spring

2 September

I'm put out with the weather. Last night was most promising: cold, late in the evening, with a mist coming down. Then today it got quite hot. Only 22°, as it turned out, but in the car, at lunchtime, it seemed far hotter. The heat had that relentless summer feel about it. It's one of those days when you think, 'That's it. Summer's here.' Between one day and the next, the woollen jumper you were grateful for a week ago becomes insufferably scratchy and suffocating.

I'd worn layers of light clothing, in any case, because I was working in the State Archives. They're situated upstairs from the Battye Library, on a sort of mezzanine floor just under the roof. The hot air rises and settles under the ceiling there. The staff work in shirt sleeves, even in the depths of winter. I was down to my T-shirt in no time.

The work is interesting. There was a typhoid epidemic in Cottesloe in the 1890s, when the suburb was first being settled, that was kept very quiet. It's been hard to trace, but the local health records, which I finally found today, are full of information. No wonder historians like to read detective fiction for pleasure. It's a busman's holiday.

3 September

It rained heavily last night, and today has been a mixture of rain and sunny periods. Warm, though; warmer than I like. If it's too hot for a jumper, then it's too hot for me.

Driving up Park Road this morning, I saw my first green parrot of the season, working its way along the verges. A number of houses share the same lawnmowing service and the grass had just been cut. The parrot's plumage was gleaming enamel. He looked as though he'd just been created. Like the horses in Dylan Thomas' poem, 'Fern Hill':

In the first, spinning place, the spell
        bound horses
walking warm
    Out of the whinnying green stable
    On to the fields of praise.

Laurie called me out just now to see a flock
of pelicans over the house. High, circling,
riding the air. Their wings were barely
moving. There were nine of them, and they
kept the same formation, even though each
individual bird's position kept changing.

Mark has been reading about flocking
behaviour. It was always assumed that
birds must have a concept of the whole
flock in order to move through the air in a
group as they do. But now it has proved
possible, with computers, to persuade
images to flock by giving them only a few
key instructions. *Don't stray too far. Don't
bump into anyone else. Don't get too cold.*

Last week we had the tree pruners come.
The Japanese pepper needed cutting back
because it interferes with the power line
to the house, but we decided to have it
pruned radically to let more sunlight into
the front garden. The Washington navel
orange tree should benefit particularly.

It's covered in blossom.

The extra sunlight gives us possibilities for new plantings. I want to repeat the success of the crabapple walk, which is at its best right now with the roses and the jasmine in full bloom. The same combination might work on the lattice fence at the front. There is the risk, though, in repeating the same varieties, that you attract more parasites. This happened when we first moved here, and planted five azoricum jasmines. The spider mite thought all its Christmases had come at once, and the jasmines have been infested ever since.

I'd also like to try a Judas tree in the corner of the wall. Laurie wants sasanqua camellias in the front garden, and an almond tree in the corner. Negotiations are proceeding. (He must be keen on the almond tree. They attract rats and I played this card with confidence, knowing how much he hates them, but it didn't work.)

The pruners also took two branches off the robinia which were shading the mandarin tree. The back garden now seems bigger. The robinia has green tips on the ends of its branches, and one or two sprays of fresh, damp-looking leaves uncurling. The mighty jacarandas next door are bare, except for some seed pods, but ours still have their punk fronds, unkempt and yellow.

4 September

Missy's gone to the vet's for a bath. When I took her to have her hearing checked, I noticed that they groom pets there, and she is one dog that's definitely in need of grooming. (There was nothing wrong, apparently, with her ears. It's just old age, the vet thinks.)

Yesterday, I raided the bulb beds for the kitchen windowsill. In the pottery jug with the sun face on it, I now have three grand monarch jonquils, three wild freesias, five bluebells, and three daffodils: a 'Salomé', a 'Dick Cissel', and one anonymous variety with pale yellow petals and a yellowish-orange centre. (The disadvantage of buying packets of assorted, unidentified daffodil bulbs with labels which say things like 'Spring Magic!' is now apparent.)

The Salomé is yellow, and quite large, with a trumpet which is a deeper colour, more a chrome yellow. The Dick Cissel is a lighter, more watery yellow all over. Its delight is its daintiness. The flower is a third or a quarter of the usual size, and the stalk about half the usual height. One bloom flowers above another on it, the lower one bowing right down so that the other can open over its head. The overall appearance is that of a wildflower rather than a cultivar, and as such it has a very old-fashioned look. The daffodils the Wordsworths saw in 1819 were probably much like these.

I used to feel embarrassed putting the blue-bells in vases, back when I thought they were weeds. Now that I have other bulbs to bring indoors, I can see how the bluebells set them off, in their yellow and cream.

5 September

I've been to the library and checked in Stirling Macoboy's *What Flower is That?* for my Erlicheers (finished, I'm afraid). That particular bulb is not mentioned, but he explains that all jonquils are varieties of *Narcissus tazetta*, and that they are distinguished by having clusters of flowers on each stem. According to this reckoning, I may safely conclude that the Erlicheer is a jonquil. I'm planning more of them for next year.

It should be possible to order bulbs rather than relying on what the local nurseries happen to have in stock. I thought I'd make some inquiries about this when we're in Melbourne at Christmas. (The bulbs I bought this autumn all came from there.) If I buy them direct from the supplier, I will have to make sure that they are acclimatised to warmer weather. This is supposed to be the case, with bulbs sold here in Perth. Putting them in the freezer for a fortnight before planting is said to be unnecessary, nowadays. 'An old wives' tale,' the superior young man at the nursery told me in April. But it was the only way my English neighbour, Diana, could get results with hers.

It's time to make common cause with old wives, anyway. The summer that Melinda turned twelve, she came over one day and announced that she was old enough to start looking after Mark and Luke (then about seven and four). I shut my mind to the worry of leaving the three of them, and took off for the pool. (Five minutes by car to get there. Twenty doing laps. Five minutes home again. Pocket money for Melinda; and half an hour's bliss for the boys.)

This arrangement with Melinda was a godsend. It wasn't just the pool, but the women there, that I needed. Older women, with grey hair, and time to swim in the middle of the day. We never spoke, but they'd nod to me; and in my fancy it seemed to me that they knew I'd come among them to be mended. I did my convalescing in that pool. Lap after lap.

Luke has gone back to school. A get well card from his teacher arrived yesterday, mentioning *en passant* that a sausage sizzle was planned for today. It did the trick.

7 September

I spent the day pruning the plumbago. It rained for long periods: a fine, silky rain that was easy to work in. In between, though, the sun was warm; and the air smelled of dust and steam the way it does in summer if there's rain.

Plumbago is back in fashion. When we first came to Perth, its blue flowers were a marvel to our Melbourne eyes. We didn't realise that plumbago was an embarrassment. It was the sort of plant people remembered from their aunty's front wire fence. The local nursery did not even stock it. We took ours as a cutting from somewhere else. Now hedges are popular again, and plumbago has been rehabilitated. There are pots and pots of it at the nursery.

8 September

Everything takes so *long*. Pruning the plumbago, for instance, I'd expected to be the work of an hour at most; instead it took me all day yesterday. Weeding occupied most of the day today.

Plants take their time, too. The freesias I planted around the base of the frangipani near the front step have been about to flower for a week. I keep willing them to open, and expecting that the next burst of sunshine will do it. It's the same with the tulips. I can't bear the waiting.

I chose yellow and white freesias, to foreshadow the yellow and white petals of the frangipani to follow. The colour of the tallest and most robust of the freesias is already evident — and it is unmistakably mauve.

This burst of pruning and weeding is the result not of any sudden access of virtue but of our quarterly collection of household rubbish being due. I've put the boys' dinky out with everything else, in the hope that a child will see it. The pedal car went to Rozzy's Giles, who's as crazy about cars as ever Mark was, but the little three-wheeled trike was too battered to give away. It's been lying about the garden, unused, for more than ten years.

9 September

The trike went last night. A woman jogger rang the bell at dusk and asked if she could take it for a little boy she knows. I didn't speak to her: Mark answered the door.

Mark says that only he rode the trike. By the time Luke was able to, he was too big for it; and the same with the car. So it's been lying around the garden for a lot longer than ten years. I'm pleased a child will have it again.

The variety of daffodil seen by Wordsworth is known to have been *Narcissus pseudonarcissus*, or 'Lent lilies', an English meadow flower, and they were almost wiped out in the Lake District because of the popularity of his poem.

I finally bought a flower book on Friday. It has a different, or rather a more extensive, set of criteria for distinguishing daffodils from jonquils. The multiple clusters of flowers, as opposed to a single trumpet, is only one of the possible ways of doing it, though it is the customary method in Australia. In England, too, the name jonquils is reserved for cluster-flowered species. In America, however, they tend to go by colour, with all the yellow ones being jonquils and all the white ones, narcissi.

Roger Mann, from whose *Ultimate Book of Flowers* this information comes, specifically mentions Narcissus Erlicheer, giving it high praise, with 'its flowers as perfect (and nearly as sweetly scented) as gardenias.' Though he identifies it as a variety of *Narcissus tazetta*, he nevertheless calls it a daffodil rather than a jonquil. (I'm going to have to let this go.)

The foliage on the pomegranate tree next to the front verandah looks as though it has been burnished. It's turned green now, but a few weeks ago the new leaves were reddish bronze, and the tree still has a coppery tinge. We transplanted it long ago from round the back. We'd taken the precaution of asking our agriculturalist friend whether it could be moved; but then we went ahead, without waiting to hear from him. A day later, he rang with an urgent warning not to move it on any account. Pomegranates have a very deep taproot, which would have to be cut, and this would kill it. Too late! There had indeed been a huge central root, which we had chopped off with abandon. Somehow the tree survived.

Just along from it there's a little stick, which was bare all winter, and which I'd assumed to be the dead remains of something Laurie had planted. It now has a crown of orange and green leaves, announcing itself to be another pomegranate.

10 September

Wonderful, wild weather. A cold,

wintry day. I thought we'd seen the last of such days.

I need to ring Jim, to tell him how good his marmalade was.

13 September

The McCartney roses are in full flower now. I can see them, and the cascades of jasmine intertwined with them, from my study window. They look like a photograph in a gardening book: too beautiful to be true.

The bees are all over the roses, scrambling clumsily across the stamens. 'Busy' is not the right word for them. They are frantic, though not as frantic as they used to be when Melinda's parents kept bees. David and Diana started out with one hive in their front garden, but ended up with three, because the bees kept swarming (once, memorably, under our Japanese pepper). David used to have to go round to the neighbours' gardens and bring them back. The honey was delicious. I've never tasted honey so fine in flavour. The bees became very distressed, though, because the hives were too close together, and according to

David they couldn't divide up the neighbourhood territory properly.

Still, they never harmed any of us. The only person to get stung was the boy up the road, who used to run a stick along the paling fence outside. Diana warned him not to do it, but he kept on. Diana had great respect for her bees.

15 September

The stormy weather began on Friday afternoon. It was another of the too-warm days that I don't like. Then, late in the day, the drop in temperature which usually occurs at about that time was accompanied by the wind starting to rise, and the wind was warm. Rain had been forecast, but very little fell. The gusts of wind became faster, and more frequent. Last night they reached gale force and one of our garage windows blew out. Today the sky is a looming, luminous grey-white. The wind and rain are battering the trees and the house, but it's not that cold. This is the first of the equinoctial storms that generally blow through in March and September.

Trevor, Luke's friend, is away at a school camp for the weekend, which gave Luke the chance to go to Claremont by himself. I dropped him at the video shop near Hungry Jack's yesterday morning with my heart in my mouth. It wasn't that the storm was bad, because there was a quiet spell about then; it was more the fear of his being run over. His eyesight is reasonably good in itself, but he can't tell distance, and he can't see anything that isn't directly in front of him.

He was home in an hour. The novelty never wears off for me. Each time he walks in the door safely is as wonderful as the first.

Some days I worry more than others.

17 September

The first tulip has flowered! It's white. Perhaps its lack of colour is what confused me. I've been waiting and watching it for weeks. I began to think that it was deformed: that there was no flower inside the calyx. I peeped in, when I got too impatient to wait any longer, and there was nothing there except for a few sickly green stamens.

I've been feeling mortified. Then, as it grew to full tulip size, and stayed green, I decided that there must be some ingredient you're supposed to put in the soil to make them colour. Overnight it has turned into a white tulip. It's perfectly shaped, and queenly looking.

Yesterday, there was almost no wind. The sky was overcast but it cleared quite early, and the rest of the day was sunny. I think that helped the tulip. I also think I may have been confused by the fact that I was expecting a red tulip, or a yellow one, because those were the two colours I planted (or thought I planted).

I'm pleased I trusted my instincts yesterday and put a load of washing out. Today there is a lot of wind, and rain is forecast. I don't know whether to leave my tulip outside at the mercy of the weather, or bring it indoors.

The freesias around the bottom of the frangipani are flowering well. I cut the mauve flower and put it in the jug in the kitchen, where I now have my third collection of daffodils, wild freesias and bluebells. After I'd cut it, though, I was sorry, because the rest of the freesias, which are white and yellow as planned, do not look as effective without a contrasting colour. So I'm pleased today to see another mauve one coming up. Next year I won't try to organise nature quite so much. I'll choose all the colours of freesia that I can find.

The top branches of the Seville are so thick with blossom that they appear to be encrusted with pearls: the whitest pearls imaginable. Further along the brick walk, the shrub called Yesterday, Today and Tomorrow (*Brunfelsia bonodora*) has come into flower. It flowers much earlier than I thought.

We've begun renovating the garage. The back verandah is covered with painted planks of wood, which are drying, as well as groundsheets, mosquito wire, and Laurie's circular saw, which shouldn't be there. (I don't know what the mosquito wire is for.)

I've been wearing my summer tracksuit pants — because despite the stormy weather it's still a lot warmer than it was — and Missy gets excited every time I go outside. These are the pants I usually wear when I take her for a walk, and she isn't above a bit of emotional blackmail. I haven't been walking her regularly for months.

I haven't been swimming, either.

20 September

Three racemes from the robinia — white, sweetly scented, like pea flowers — are lying on the verge under the tree. I couldn't see any in the tree itself, even with the branches bare.

I looked up and up, into the brightest of blue skies, searching until I got giddy. Meanwhile, the honeyeaters continued to wage the Battle of Britain around me, dive-bombing Missy, chasing off the pair of crows that's moved in, and hurtling hell-for-leather after an outraged green parrot.

Pink everlastings are crowding along the boundaries of the cemetery. The Thomas Street side of Kings Park is dense with freesias. They are thickest where the last fire was.

21 September

Last Monday evening, at about dusk, I lay down for half an hour to rest. While I was lying there, resisting the temptation to read, I slowly began to feel better. The demands of the day receded. The very wardrobes and cupboards, which seemed to be looming over me when first I lay down, slowly stepped back, one by one, and gave me space. I glimpsed a possible life for myself. I felt the spaciousness of it.

In the warmth, the smell of the orange blossom in the front garden hangs heavily in the air. You really notice it as you come in the gate. Mark sits on the verandah to study. The bulb pots, though, are beginning to look like neglected funerary urns. There is a second tulip flowering, and another Dick Cissel about to come out, but that's all, apart from the freesias, which are doing reasonably well (two shades of yellow at present). Some of the bulbs in the other pots sprouted but didn't flower. Others, like the pheasant's eye daffodils, haven't come up at all. Only one blue iris ever came out, which leaves two pots of bare earth, with strips of silvery green hanging down, at the end of the row. The grand monarch jonquils, which did so well in the ground, haven't flowered in the pots though they look healthy enough.

I think it's probably too late for them now. There can't have been sufficient sun along there, after all. That side of the brick walk looks like a necropolis.

This weekend I want to begin writing about what life was like in Cottesloe at the turn of the century, if you were poor. (There's not a made bed in the house. The bathroom is a shambles. I'm so far behind with the washing that the dirty laundry is about to overflow into the clean clothes that are waiting to be ironed.)

It's lunchtime. The wind is starting to lift.

24 September

The car is at the panel beater's. Being without it is like being a student again. I know the novelty will wear off all too soon, as it did in London, but for the moment it feels like freedom. Yesterday was the same. I suppose it's partly the relief of casting off the shackles of normal life. Almost every commitment in my diary has had to be cancelled because the pace of my life cannot be sustained without a car. (So much for having slowed down since my thirties!)

Added to this is the knowledge that I don't have to be back at a particular time for the kids. I worked until 6.30 yesterday evening, and came home on the train. It was dark by then. Seen from the unaccustomed angle of the train window, the familiar streets looked completely foreign. I could have been in another city.

I'm making all sorts of resolutions about getting about more on foot. Heavenly time I'm having, in the meantime.

25 September

A shawl of silvery-grey was enveloping the sky as I rode along Thomas Street on the bus this morning. It was the colour and texture of pussy willows, but corrugated, like corduroy, and spreading slowly southwards.

Breakfast in town.

26 September

There's sunlight streaming in through the bedroom windows at seven each morning, and I wake in fear that I've overslept.

27 September

The front step is alight with freesias and Dick Cissel daffodils (one of them with *three* trumpets on it!).

It poured with rain all day yesterday. *How* one welcomes it! The steaminess in the air (though the day was colder, it was still not a wintry cold) is a reminder, nevertheless, that the earth, the plants, and we ourselves, will soon be thirsting in vain.

Perhaps this year will be different. A few weeks ago, Mundaring Weir overflowed at last. It was the first time that this had happened for more than twenty years. Before the current dry cycle (which may last another decade, according to some geographers), the dam used to overflow every two or three winters. It was almost a routine occurrence. Not this time. Tens of thousands of people are driving up to

Mundaring each weekend to see it. It's like a pilgrimage. That scalloped veil of white water, sliding elegantly across the face of the dam, is a matter for awe.

Last night there were two claps of thunder, and some lightning. The rain came in sudden, heavy bursts. Towards ten, when I went to bed, the sky was pale and gleaming, because the moon is full. It's sunny again this morning, but there's a vast mushroom-coloured cloud hanging low towards the east. I don't know if it's advancing or receding.

28 September

Sebastian has been leading a double life. We always knew that he spent a lot of time at Ernie's, two doors down. When we lose him he's generally to be found there. And we knew that, being banned from our garden, he had made next door's his own. Lately he's been defending that territory from a new grey cat, who's much younger. This has involved keeping watch from the smaller of the two jacaranda trees in their back garden. It's outside our laundry window, and he calls tragically to us while he's on duty.

The battlefield proper is the roof of the house next door. It has a gentle slope; the trees shade part of it; elsewhere, it's sunny and warm. Perfect for a tired cat. But every so often the grey cat nonchalantly happens by, appearing out of nowhere over the ridge, and the yowling starts. There's a lot more yowling than actual contact, but Sebastian still crawls home with a nasty cut every few weeks.

Now, though, we're wondering whether our house *is* home to him. The kids who live next door moved in as students some years ago. Laurie taught the sister when she was an undergraduate. She, her brother Paul, and their friends, have come and gone over the years. Last weekend, I noticed furniture tied to trailers on the verge, and found out from Paul that he's moving back in.

The surprise was that he and everyone else in the house have been feeding Sebastian — 'not *constantly*, but regularly' — for *ten years*, ever since they first came here: 'He's a terrific cat.' Paul didn't even know that Sebastian belonged to us. It reminds me of the time long ago when I saw him in ecstasy on the front wall, writhing and rolling, purring fit to burst, and answering to the name of 'Circus'.

The car may be ready this afternoon. Luke's school holidays start today, and he's keen to meet the man at the repair shop, so the plan is that he and I will go down to Fremantle by bus late today and collect the car, if it's ready.

I do hope it is. The big weekend shop is looming, for Laurie; and Monday is a public holiday. Added to which, I'm supposed to be making a Christmas cake. The prunes have been soaking in rum for a fortnight, but I haven't bought the other ingredients. Sue said she would drive me to the supermarket, but so far we haven't both been free at the same time. It's my grandmother's recipe, and even for one cake the weight of fruit is considerable. I wouldn't want to carry it home on foot.

My middle name is Mary, after her. She was my father's mother, not my Greek grandmother (who died before I was born). My grandmother Hopping lived at Ingleburn in all the years I knew her, but she'd grown up in the far west of New South Wales. She cooked her whole life on a wood stove, and her cakes were legion. The fruit cake recipe was much in demand for wedding cakes. Someone else would ice them: she didn't do that. She died when Mark was getting on for a year old. She never knew him, but she did see photographs. She took one look at that Graeco-Italian face and said, 'I don't think he's a Hopping!' She would have been eighty-four then. Her birthday's in July, like mine.

The lavender has been in flower for at least a month. It's responded very well to being trimmed: all except one bush, which I cut back to about a third of its former size. It was wild and straggly, with large bare patches. It is looking very healthy, with lots of new green growth, but I guess it may not flower for another year.

The tall white jug with the grey cupid pattern has *eight* arum lilies in it. They've been there for about a week. Each day they have been leaning a little closer towards each other, and now they curve upwards together in a single arc.

The cloud seems to be clearing, but there's a bitingly cold draft driving under the door of this room. I might be able to get a load of washing dry.

29 September

Noon. A sudden staccato roar from what sounded like an armed squad of kookaburras somewhere down the lane. I had a quick look for them in the row of jacarandas along there, but I couldn't see a single one, even though the branches are all bare. Four or five smaller birds were scattering fast.

On Friday night, Luke suggested that he should start to tuck himself in as he is 'going to be a grown-up' soon. I was delighted not to have to get up. There's been nothing worse at the end of the day, for years and years, than to have to leave a TV programme, or put down a book, in order to settle him. But last night, lying in bed, after he'd managed alone for the second time, I felt a pang. Before I fully realised what I was doing, I found myself thinking up ways of reinstating our ritual: perhaps by saving it for certain days of the week. 'Goodnight. Sleep tight. See you in the morning light.' And then in recent years, with the influence of American movies, a coda: *'Don't let the bedbugs bite!'*

The viburnums in the front garden have responded with gusto to the trimming of the Japanese pepper. The viburnum is sometimes called 'the wayfarer's tree'. According to Roger Mann, this name should properly be applied only to *Viburnum lantana*, a European species, but it's such an evocative 'Song of the Open Road' sort of name that I'm not prepared to give it up. There are at least a hundred species, and they come from North America and Asia, as well as England and Europe.

We have two examples of *Viburnum burkwoodii* (named after an English nursery-man) by the lattice fence, and both are gloriously in flower. Scented white snow-balls tinged with pink: there must be at least a dozen of them on each bush. I've never seen more than three previously. Near them, against the wall, *Viburnum tinus*, an evergreen variety, is covered with clusters of coral pink berries. It comes from southern Europe. Under the lounge room window, another evergreen variety, this time from Japan, has finished flowering, and is also sporting berries — though they are not as noticeable — in a slightly paler shade. Even Laurie, who in the past would have been more likely to pay attention than I, has never seen berries on these shrubs before.

(Added to which, according to Walter Hazlewood, *Viburnum japonicum* should produce berries in autumn, not spring.)

The weeping mulberry is slowly coming into leaf, but only on the inside of the wall. The bottom tips of its branches have leaves which are almost full-sized, but they get smaller and smaller as they go up. The top half is still quite bare, as are all the branches on the outside of the wall.

Another vase of spring flowers, this time on my desk. A white tulip, some white and some lemon-coloured freesias, a magenta one, a purple anemone, and two yellow daffodils.

The day is sunny and hot, but there are overcast patches, and when it's cloudy you notice the chill of the wind. Laurie leaves for Italy tomorrow.

1 October

You're encouraged to stimulate your baby, and you do. You're trained as a teacher, there's *no one* you can't teach. You've never failed before. There's nothing you can't do.

Oh, he was engaging. Fetching and carrying, like any toddler, he brought me cookbooks, toys, bits of food, and dishes. Laurie, on the other hand, got men's stuff: string, sticky tape, his cigarettes. One of my aunts, despatched from Sydney when Luke was four, to get me to come to my senses and put him permanently in care, was stopped in her tracks by the sight of him.

Not for an instant, not for a nanosecond, did it occur to me that there might be nothing *anyone* could do.

4 October

At the hairdresser's, the girl who used to dye my hair is getting distressed about the grey. She must have thought it was a temporary lapse. How to explain the liberation it's been to let the colour go? Nothing and nobody will make me change it back.

She can't be more than twenty. In fact, I know she's Mark's age, because one Christmas, when I'd run out of ideas for him, she told me exactly what to get and she was exactly right. (Aftershave from the Body Shop. A CD voucher in a CD gift box. A *good* T-shirt.)

Luke and Trevor are going to see *The Phantom* at the Windsor and then having a late lunch at Pizza Hut. I'll be driving them, but I'm planning to show them how to get the bus back afterwards, so that they can start learning a new route together now that their trips to town seem to be passing off without a hitch. Trevor only needs to be shown once. He's also in charge of road crossing. Luke's a good reader (useful for menus), and he does the timekeeping.

All that walking last week has got me going again. I've started taking Missy out, in defiance of the nesting magpies and the honeyeaters. One magpie swooped on me this morning but as a token gesture rather than a real attack. It shot back up on to the telephone wire and did a victory chortle. Hard to resist the impression that they *know* they can get away with it at this time of year.

I have much more trouble with the honeyeaters, even though it's Missy they're after. As long as you can hear their harsh warning rasp, you're safe. When they plunge, like magpies they're utterly silent. The first you know of it is the flurry of wings against your cheek. I find them terrifying. (Missy, oblivious, trots steadily on.)

Luke's going to Landsdale for the second week of the holidays. I can't wait.

5 October

'I can't wait' is not quite what I meant. It's more that I can't wait to be on my own. I'm looking forward to five days by myself, since Laurie's away as well. He goes to Italy for a month every year to do archival research, and spends most of the time in Florence. Mark will be home, but he's in the Medical Library a lot now — 'I can't study in this house' — and anyway he can make his own meals.

I'm planning to spend my time totally the way I want. An uninterrupted week on the Cottesloe material. The Kandinsky exhibition. Walks with Missy. *Swimming.* And I've been stockpiling books since the middle of September.

The smallest of the Orange jessamines has flowered. We have three. One is slightly different from the others, so it may be that we have both *Murraya exotica* and *Murraya paniculata*. The names appear interchangeably on their nursery labels, and they are hard to tell apart. *Murraya paniculata* could possibly be a variety of *Murraya exotica*, it's thought. They come from the tropical parts of Australia, Asia, and the Pacific Islands.

I assumed from the name that it must originally have grown along the banks of the Murray River, but in fact the shrub is named after an eighteenth-century professor of botany, J A Murray. Murray edited the works of the renowned Linnaeus, whose *Systema Naturae*, published in 1735, established the principles of plant classification which are still in use today. Linnaeus greatly revered his predecessor, Micheli, and dedicated the genus *Michelia* to him.

I first smelled Orange jessamine in Toodyay last year. Walking down from where I was staying, towards the town, there was a large flowering shrub whose perfume wafted up the hill. It was in the front garden of an old house, and dense with bees. It looked as though it had been there forever. I brought back a sprig of it, and at Dawson's nursery they identified it for me. Home I came in triumph, with two tiny pots, to find that we already had one, planted by Laurie some time before. (It's one of *my* plants that's flowering, though.) The shrub seems to be very slow growing. (Laurie's is only just beginning to develop and mine are the same size they were when we put them in.) It blossoms in spring and summer. The Toodyay one shouldn't have been flowering in July.

In Toodyay, the gravel road next to the railway line is covered with grazing galahs in the morning. You see cars slow down and swing around them. The galahs don't move.

I've never seen so many. There are two tall gums where they roost. They come shrieking in at dusk, flock after flock, hundreds of them, and each time a new group arrives there are fights. All the birds fly up, screaming, and then they slowly settle, with much squabbling, until the next lot arrives. Those gums are Dickensian tenements.

Toodyay may not have been the first occasion on which I smelled that shrub. It had an old-fashioned look to me, and Orange jessamine has been popular in

Sydney for a very long time. I wonder whether perhaps I knew it in childhood, from visiting my aunts.

6 October

The warmest day so far. The temperature must be in the mid twenties. The plants are starting to wilt: and not only those in pots. The two young fig trees also need watering. Argentine ants are swarming on the back gate. I don't know why I thought that taking the duck away would deter them. They must simply have transferred themselves to a place of greater safety. When Luke came in from walking the dog, covered in winged ants, I went straight out and sprayed them. I was impressed at my lack of compunction.

We've lived in Perth for the whole of this dry cycle — if dry cycle it be, and not the latter days of global warming — but I've never got used to the way the rainy season ends so abruptly. Days and then weeks go by before you slowly become aware that the last fall of rain, whenever it was — you never remember exactly when — truly was just that. If I knew it was to be the last, how

I would cherish it — dance naked in it — say to myself, Remember this! (The way the air smells different beforehand. The feel of the rain on your skin.)

Claire over the road has had her sixteenth birthday party. She lives where Melinda used to. Her mother came over to let me know in advance because she was worried about the noise — 'Just say to yourself, "It will all be over at 11.30!"' — but in fact there was no loud music. Lots of exuberant shrieking, though, as the evening wore on. Gail very sensibly insisted on staying, but Wayne took the younger kids out so that Claire wouldn't feel too oppressed. Judging by the squeals this morning, I'd say some of the girls slept over. When I heard them, I felt a pang of envy. The post-mortems were always so much better than the actual party.

On the morning after cracker night, when we lived in Brisbane, my brother and I would go out at first light in our slippers searching in the damp grass for fireworks that hadn't gone off; and Dad would split them open and light them for us. Whether it was the thrill of the search, or the fact of getting our hands on the crackers — if only briefly before we handed them over to be lit

— I don't know, but it was far more fun than the night before.

I think it was because cracker night itself was frightening. You had to stand well back, and the bangs were terrifying. The sizzling squibs next morning were more friendly.

7 October

Started watering in earnest this morning, after taking Missy for a walk. Laurie's Spanish broom is coming into flower.

Then I drove Luke to his camp at Lands-dale. Felt terribly flat afterwards. I never remember this feeling ahead of time, but it always comes, and it always hits hard. I'm so focussed on getting him packed and ready, while concealing from him the fun I'm going to have on my own, that I forget the pall that descends straight away.

Driving back down the Wanneroo Road, I had to keep reminding myself that if I don't have these breaks I can't keep going. Then I thought of stopping at the Re Store to get some gorgonzola for the pasta sauce I'm working on. The recipe I learned in Parma in the 1970s was for equal quantities of gorgonzola and farm butter. It got a bit oily as we got older, so I switched to Laurie's sister's recipe which uses half as much gorgonzola as fontina, a light Italian cheese, and only a sliver of butter. Now I'm working on a variation of my own, basing the sauce on Laurie's mother's recipe for broad beans. You cook the beans for about an hour with a chopped onion, two chopped tomatoes, peas, and a little oil and water. (She adds fresh artichoke hearts, too.) Then you add the cooked vegetables to the sauce, which is the same as Anna's, more or less, except that I'm now adding cream, to thin it a little, and a bit of grated parmesan.

The first time I made it, it was a wild success. I tried again yesterday, but something went wrong. I think the cream curdled because the melted cheese was too hot.

Laurie's going to be so pleased about the Spanish broom. It is *Spartium junceum*, a species all of its own, though it closely resembles the other types of broom. The word *junceum*, which means rush-like, refers to the branches, which have no leaves. The more conservative gardening books say to prune it after flowering, but I don't think Laurie will want to; and apparently, if you don't prune it, it tends to develop a starker, more interesting shape. He remembers hillsides covered in it, from his childhood.

The smallgoods section of the Re Store has a cathedral-like atmosphere. Recipes are reverently exchanged. *'Io ci metto prezzemolo, aglio ...'* Parsley, garlic; intense concentration on both sides of the counter.

It was the man at the Re Store who taught me a sauce for filled pasta. I was buying beef tortellini to cook with shredded chicken and a béchamel sauce, but he told me to try them his way. The basic sauce of tinned Italian tomatoes and chopped fried onion (no garlic), cooked for forty-five minutes, is finished with enough cream to turn it a coral colour, and plenty of minced flat-leaved parsley. It's good with ravioli as well, especially the spinach ones.

(Regarding the beef tortellini. The version with chicken comes from Ada Boni, the title of whose encyclopaedic work, *Il talismano della felicità*, says all it's necessary to say about Italians and their love of food. You bake the cooked pasta and béchamel sauce in the oven, with parmesan cheese and butter on top. To the man at the Re Store it may be an outlandish northern recipe, but served with a plain green salad, it is truly wonderful.)

8 October

It was 31° yesterday. The beginning of the heat. Nevertheless, there are compensations. The loquat tree up the road, for example: the pale orange of the fruit against the emerald green breasts of the parrots feasting on it. And outside Sally's this morning, when I dropped by to return her tape, the sight of a group of four small children trying to catch a white butterfly. The boy last in line cupped one of Sally's Flanders poppies in his hand, gazed at it intently, face to face, then gently let it go.

If it weren't for my dread of the heat, I could enjoy this balmy weather. It's never hot for long, the days are spiked with strong sea breezes, and the nights are cool.

The first of the iris orchids is out today. It was a former neighbour's grandmother's plant. A pot was passed on to her when she married, and she gave me a shoot from it. It's not an orchid at all, actually, but 'Neomarica', a rhizome, belonging to the vast family of *Iridaceae*. Because it spreads by means of its flowers re-rooting themselves in the ground, it's often called the walking iris, but to Margot's grandmother it was an iris orchid, and that's the name we've given it, to remember her by.

Stirling Macoboy is scathing about Neo-marica in *What Flower is That?* Because its flowering span is so short, he says that it has curiosity value only. He's certainly right about the flowers lasting no more than a day. They don't survive in water, either. But for the few days that it blooms, the iris orchid shimmers above the green depths of its leaves like a mirage. Ours is in the typical iris shape of a fleur-de-lis. The petals of the outer trefoil are white, while those inside are the deepest violet blue. They smell faintly of attar of roses, and they look like an Arthur Rackham drawing.

10 October

A grey, windy morning. More huff and puff than rain, but there were a few showers in the night, and more are promised for today.

11 October

Great day with Jo Trevelyan. Not that we did any work.

18 October

One (just one) of the Salomé daffodils has flowered. I wish there were more. It's in a specimen vase on my desk, and so delicate. Greenish-white outer petals, with a trumpet whose base is the same colour as the petals, but whose outer edge — the most noticeable feature of the flower — is crinkly in shape and pale peach in colour. There doesn't appear to be any scent.

What I'm going to have to do with the bulbs is to fertilise them all now, and let the leaves die down; and then lift them, and try again next year. I think the problem was not enough sun. Maybe I should also have put them in a bit earlier. I'm tempted to empty the pots and throw all the duds away, but I think it's worth another try. The leaves look so healthy! The only other possibility I can think of is that the drainage in the pots may not have been good enough. When I exhume the bulbs, I should be able to tell if they've rotted.

I'm moving the pots to the back of the garden so that the leaves can die down in peace. (You are absolutely not allowed to cut them off, despite their unsightliness.) This will leave fewer pots along the brick walk. My previous plan was to replace the bulbs immediately with lavender, but we'll be away for six weeks at Christmas; the new plants would be needing extra attention at the very time we won't be here. It would be more sensible to wait until the summer is over. This would also mean better care for the existing plants, since we're stretched to our limit as it is. They're already short of water, particularly the gardenias under the eaves.

One of the gardenias very nearly died two summers ago. The heat was bad, and Laurie's parents were here, so he was concentrating on them rather than the garden.

It was a matter of a day or two, but almost too late by the time we noticed.

Luke went back to school on Tuesday after the holidays, which is when Jo and I went out for coffee to celebrate. She introduced me to *citron pressé*, which they do at the Subiaco Dome, and which I'd only ever read about.

I've decided to try making it. I've squeezed all the lemons that were in the fruit bowl and made up the sugar syrup, using caster sugar and an equal quantity of water. I still have to get the sparkling mineral water. In Italy everyone drinks mineral water because the tap water's so bad, and you can buy it cheaply in huge packs like we do pallets of soft drink cans.

The plan is to sit out on the verandah all summer, drinking *citrons pressés* and gazing at the garden.

21 October

Yesterday, the temperature was already 28° at nine am when I went to put the washing out. The violets under the mandarin tree were exhausted.

The day got very hot. The temperature reached nearly 37°: a seventeen-year record for October. Then there was a sudden waft of Chinese star jasmine from the wall outside. I've been watching it like a hawk for weeks, but still I missed the moment when it flowered. Beforehand, its glossy green leaves get the bronzed look of a plant that's dying. This is a sign that it's about to flower. About three weeks later a faint white scrim covers the vine, formed by the pricks of its star-shaped buds.

As each scented plant comes into bloom, I think, 'This is my favourite', but *Trachelospermum jasminoides* — 'jasmine-*like*': it's not a true jasmine — is probably my keenest delight. It comes from Southern China.

Then last night I heard the rain. Thundery showers had been predicted, but they often don't eventuate, or are so light, and the earth so warm, that the water evaporates in a steaming instant as soon as it touches the ground. But this was different. It rained all night: steady, soaking rain, and it hasn't stopped yet (at nearly nine on Monday morning). I've had time to lift my eyes and see that the Sparrieshoop is laden with pink roses: more than I've ever seen. The weather's stayed warm — I'm writing this in my T-shirt — but all the windows and doors are open, and headlong draughts of rain-drenched air are racing through the house.

All three pomegranate trees are dotted with bright red buds. There are never very many, and this year is typical: about fifteen buds on the two older trees, and five on the youngest. The little sapling has put out another stalk from its base. It's knee-height now, but bowed nearly to the ground by the weight of the rainwater. Laurie doesn't want it staked, though I'd like to give it a helping hand. It will be stronger, I know, if left to itself.

22 October

The whole house is filled with the scent of the jasmine. Heady spring days. Days to swim in.

There are yellow trumpet flowers on one of the vines on the lattice fence. It seems to be the cat's claw creeper, which has stealthily climbed up the crêpe myrtle without our noticing, strangled it, and produced these large bright flowers in triumph.

This vine hasn't flowered before. Is it another beneficiary of the extra sunlight pouring into that part of the garden, because of the cut back Japanese pepper? The bauhinia in the corner hasn't gained anything. It's hardly flowered at all and is looking every bit as scrawny and yellow as usual. The scrawniness is our fault, because we haven't pruned it, but the burnt look of the leaves is characteristic of our particular variety (*Bauhinia variegata*) after the winter. This does not stop me gnashing my teeth at the spectacular appearance of all the other bauhinias in the gardens round about us, especially the white ones. (Ours is purple: a mistake on the nursery's part. Laurie had ordered a white one.)

This spring we have a magpie who is a dedicated songster. He works away, perfecting every liquid trill, mostly in the middle of the morning but sometimes in the late afternoon as well. I haven't seen him yet, but he's a joy to hear. I'm flattered he's chosen our garden.

The cat's claw creeper was my idea. In past years, whenever we'd go to the nursery to pick up a scented species that Laurie had ordered, I'd occupy myself with buying whatever caught my eye (which would inevitably be whatever was in flower at the time). Most of my choices died quite promptly, but some have lived to infest the garden.

More rain is predicted.

23 October

Sebastian may have turned back the tide. For about a month he's only come inside to snatch a quick bite in the evening, and then it's been out again into the fray. He's moved the battlefield a rooftop further away. I don't know how everyone's putting up with the noise at night. It's bad even from here. The neighbours are probably feeling as guilty as we are, since they all seem to think he's their cat. We've tried to keep him in at night but he's too old to change his ways.

25 October

It's warming up again.

27 October

Sebastian has taken to sleeping on the verge in a cubbyhole made by the branches of the weeping mulberry, which hang right down to the ground. And I've seen the grey cat cautiously working its way towards what used to be Sebastian's favourite spot on next door's roof, above their front porch where the branches of an enormous hibiscus give cover. Has Sebastian lost ground, after all?

28 October

This morning, Jo and I sat on the front verandah and talked about our future lives. (We're only a month apart in age.) There's nothing stopping either of us now with whatever we want to do. It's not that we don't know how lucky we both are even to be able to contemplate a fresh start. What's making it hard is not knowing whether we'll succeed, and having to wait until we're sixty, at least, to find out. (And it's not that we're *really* beginning all over again.)

We drank *citrons pressés*. The dregs, actually, of my second batch, because Mark and his friends have fallen on it like wolves. The combination of lemon juice, sugar syrup and mineral water in the fridge, all at the same time, may never be achieved again. (The first batch of syrup was too dense and sank to the bottom of the glass. Two cups of water to every one of sugar works better.)

My aunts and my mother-in-law, all in their eighties, laugh when I speak of sixty as old.

29 October

The 'Blue Moon' rose is in bud. You may prune it, water it, fertilise it as you will: the result will always be seven flowers per annum, no more; and the distinct feeling that you should be offering formal congratulations. A telegram from the Queen, perhaps. It's such a prima donna of a plant.

A letter has come from Judy. When I was young, I couldn't have imagined something as simple as a letter bringing such joy. Now a letter from a friend floods the day with light.

30 October

A hot night last night. Not a breath of air, though I had every window in the house open, in anticipation of the thunderstorms which were forecast, but never came.

Sebastian hasn't been in for two nights. I heard him crying early today in the jacaranda tree next door. He has taken up his sentry post again.

31 October

I first saw the blue moon rose in Aunty Myrtle's garden at Ealing. She'd ordered it from the Chelsea Flower Show. That would be twenty-five years ago now: it must have been a new rose then.

The colour is a bluish mauve, and the scent like that of a deep, velvety red rose, but lighter, almost lemony. It would be churlish to begrudge this rose its histrionics.

1 November

The forecast rain did not come yesterday. Instead, it slipped away south to the Bight. All we've been left with is the humidity.

It's some compensation to be able to sleep with the bedroom windows wide open. The easterly wind comes straight in, and it's cool at night. Sleeping with the windows open is the particular gift of this season.

There are three mangoes on the lemon-decorated plate Mark gave me for my birthday. Laurie's favourite fruit, awaiting his return.

2 November

The bigger of the two jacarandas next door has its first flowers opening. It's a giant: almost as high as our robinia. Our jacarandas are looking no more promising than usual. Generally, only the middle one flowers. Each year at about this time we threaten to cut the others down if they don't start, but they seem to know we don't really mean it.

I'm back to hand watering the dichondra. Next year's oranges are setting on both trees. I must fertilise the Seville. I did the Washington navel a couple of months ago, and it's got lots of fruit.

I looked up the blue moon rose when I went to the library. It's a hybrid tea rose, developed in Germany, and first launched in 1964. Aunty Myrtle must have bought it not long afterwards. She had it in her garden by the time we arrived in London in 1971.

4 November

Laurie's brought a new sauce back from Florence, called *fiaccheraia*. It's eaten with fairly thin spaghetti. Elsewhere in Italy it goes by other names — *puttanesca, alla diavola, arrabbiata*. In Florence, however, it's named for the drivers of *fiacres* — those small, four-wheeled cabs, from the days before cars — who needed something spicy in the winter, to keep them warm.

To the usual mixture of onions and garlic, fried in olive oil and butter, you add one small fresh chilli, finely chopped, or half a dried one, and two rashers of bacon, diced.

Then the tinned tomatoes. Tomato paste will do instead (diluted with water), as long as it's *triplo concentrato*, and half an hour's simmering will 'see it done', as Eliza Acton would say. (Though not of a recipe like this! She was right, nevertheless, in her approach. The best recipes are the simple ones.)

6 November

Rain last night, continuing today. Unusual so late in the year, and a tonic for the garden. How I love this weather! With grey skies, and the sound of rain falling, I feel wrapped up and safe indoors. My family moved to Melbourne when I was six, and I lived there until Laurie and I married and went to England. Perhaps that's why I love the rain.

The honeysuckle flowered in time for Laurie's arrival. Try as we might, we've been unable to force it out of the middle pomegranate tree, from which it is now hanging in long festoons. The pomegranate looks like one of those mysterious swamp trees in the Florida Everglades.

A salmon pink oleander, which Laurie grew from a cutting, has also bloomed for the first time.

7 November

The Cottesloe report is taking a lot of time. I'm having trouble casting the material as well as I want to. This is partly the perfectionist devil on my shoulder, but partly too the difficulty of bringing a different perspective to bear upon an area which we all feel we know well. Cottesloe's history has been written and re-written, but it is largely the story of the well-to-do. What remains untold is the hardship of the early years: the 1890s, when the suburb was first settled, and the first decade of the twentieth century, when many people were living in tents, shacks and humpies. There were recurrent typhoid epidemics — erroneously blamed on outsiders — because people's wells were contaminated by cesspits. A far cry from the vision of a healthy seaside suburb which springs so readily to mind.

One baby boy drowned in the backyard chicken pen of his parents' Dalgety Street house in 1902. His eight-year-old sister was in charge of him at the time.

Mum went back to Fremantle to scrub out the quarters that we had been living in. She left the baby with me. I put him down to sleep in his cot and I washed up the lunch dishes; and then he woke up, and I took him out to the laundry where my brother and younger sisters were, and left him with them, and swept out the dining room. I was taking the crumbs and that down the backyard to the chooks — I suppose we had fowls at the bottom of the yard — and I found my baby brother. He had a red Turkey twill dress on — they used to dress the baby boys and girls in dresses like that — and he was face down. I must have screamed, because women came running out, and my brother, and they got a stick, and got it up his dress, and pulled him out, and carried him in ... I have never asked a child to kiss over a body. Mother had him laid out in a little white cot on the bed, and she told us to go and kiss him goodbye, and the shock to a child: a body that is so cold, that has always been so warm. I would never ask a child to do that; never ask anybody.

The sister was eighty-two years of age when she recounted this episode in 1976. She and her family moved from Cottesloe to Cannington almost immediately afterwards, because of the doctor's advice to her father 'to get Mum away from there.'

8 November

I've just delivered Missy to the vet's for a bath. She was supposed to go on Wednesday, but as well as being wet it was quite cold, and I was worried that she might get a chill. It's sunny again, but a mild day, with a strong sea breeze expected for this afternoon. On my way back inside after dropping her off, I checked the Caroline jasmine, and it *is* about to flower. The sweet, honey-like scent is detectable on a still night for at least a week before the flowers actually open, and I'd been thinking I could smell it, even though it was at first no more than a grace note to the heavier Chinese star jasmine, which can now be smelled a street away.

Caroline jasmine is a misnomer. It's not *Gelsemimium sempervirens*, from the Carolinas in the United States, but *Cestrum nocturnum*, from the West Indies. In its original habitat it flowers throughout the summer, but ours flowers in spring. At the very end of last summer, though, it gave us a return performance, when it perfumed the stifling nights like a benison. I cut it back carefully afterwards, because it's inclined to be leggy, and now, from the bunched look of the long, thin buds (which last year were rather sparse), I'd say it's going to bloom well. I'm already wondering greedily whether we'll get a second flowering again.

Apart from these high points, my spirits are low. I've been reading Erica Jong's biography of Henry Miller. She says how hard it was to find one voice to write it in: 'I felt as I often did when beginning one of my own novels — lost in mist, looking for a voice ... and a trail of breadcrumbs.' I feel this way about my days. This journal gives me a trail to look back upon, but it cannot mark the path ahead.

One of the hardest things for me, with Luke, was the constant fear that one more minute with him might be the very minute that would make a difference. There was no sense, ever, that the countless hours I spent engaging his attention were ever *enough*. I forgot that I was only one person.

Trish's honeysuckle is in flower as well. Though it also has white flowers fading to creamy-yellow, there are fewer of them, and the leaves are a darker green. It's the honey-suckle you see in older gardens like hers. It's a lot less fluffy looking than our other honeysuckle, and not as vigorous, but the scent is much stronger.

Yesterday afternoon, I saw Sasha's older sister at Plane Tree Farm, where she's working part-time. Sasha was Mark's best friend, from pre-school right through until the beginning of Year 4, when the two of them finally gave up trying to sustain a boy–girl friendship in the internecine world of the upper primary. Sasha is at James Cook University in Northern Queensland studying marine biology.

When I told her sister — tall and slim, with grey-blue eyes and her hair in a straight bob to her jawline — that I hadn't recognised her, she said, 'That's because I'm a grown-up!' She must be twenty-three or twenty-four. I remember when their father collected the children from school to see their baby brother being born. James is in Year 10 now, apparently, and wears his head shaved.

I'm beginning to like the American journalist P J O'Rourke. He's more of a liberal than he's prepared to admit (as I can appreciate now that I've started reading him, as distinct from condemning him unread). In his new collection of essays, he describes a Native American hunting guide, called Tom, as insisting that Indians never get lost. It's the *path* that wanders away. Maybe that's what's happened to me. The path's wandered off for a while.

15 November

In my study group yesterday, we were discussing the work of the philosopher Emmanuel Levinas. (This is my psychotherapy seminar, which meets every week. I'm in my second term.) We were debating whether human suffering can be placed on a continuum with the experience of

European Jewry during the Second World War at one extreme. I took the position summarised by Clive James in *Unreliable Memoirs*, which I've just finished re-reading, that such a comparison is self-indulgent. What we may experience, even if we are very unlucky, is no more than normal human tragedy: what James, quoting Nadezhda Mandelstam, calls 'the privilege of ordinary heartbreaks.' What happened to the Jews was not this.

I said that even though having a retarded child was the worst thing that could have happened to me — worse, by far, than the death of a child — it was still no more than an ordinary heartbreak: in Mandelstam's terms, a privilege, because it happened in the normal world. There was food on the table. Parents, sisters, brother, friends, all kept their place in the firmament. Returning to Melbourne for Christmas, we will find our small planet almost exactly as it was when we went spinning off, nearly seventeen years ago.

Saying my piece about Luke, though, I wondered how much of it was still true. I would *not* now prefer that he not outlive us. I no longer think that it would have been less unbearable to have him die: not even in the innermost part of myself, where the hope for his death used to hide.

Soon after Luke was born, I began to feel that we had been expelled from the normal world. That, to me, in those days, was the world where things didn't go wrong unless it was your own fault. Suddenly, I found myself in the abnormal world; and I didn't believe I belonged there. (After all, I'd done nothing to deserve it.) We spent the first few years of his life, to my mind, in wrongful exile.

Then it became clear that what we had entered, by virtue of Luke's disabilities, *was* the normal world. The world where paying your taxes, and being kind to people, and keeping your insurance up-to-date won't save you. The world where anything can happen. Certainty was gone from our lives.

(This was a gift.)

16 November

It's been raining for two nights. The garden is drenched in green. I feel smug about this unseasonal weather, as though it were my personal accomplishment.

The coral vine (*Russelia equisetiformis*) is starting to flower, and the Albertine rose has buds. The jacarandas are impervious to our desires. There are three small clumps of purple on the first of them, and that is all. The streets are royally bedecked with jacarandas in full flower but ours refuse to conform.

It's exactly a month until we leave for Melbourne. I can't bear to think of how much I've got to get done before we go. The Cottesloe deadline looms largest. Luke is going on a ten-day camp on Tuesday, and I simply must have the report finished by the time he returns. That will leave two weeks to organise the house, the pets and the packing. I dread *all* of it. How many days to go, I wonder, before I start confiding to this journal that the upheaval isn't worth it?

17 November

Sue rang to say that her house (which went to auction yesterday) has sold. She and her husband Phil are delighted. It overlooks the river, and they were reluctant to let it go, but their children have well and truly left home now (Matthew is in America and Emma is married) and they wanted something smaller. I'm sorry about the house, with its wide verandah, its white columns, and its view, but relieved for them.

I've got to get started on Luke's packing. His school has organised this Venture programme for Year 10. It's normally too taxing for the Special Education students, but this year two members of the support staff are giving their time to take them. We never go camping, so the world of rucksacks and hiking boots, of beanies and gloves (for bedtime), is completely foreign to me. The boys have shared ownership of a sleeping bag for years, mostly for Mark to use when he goes to stay with friends, but all the other equipment has had to be bought or hired. I'm about to see whether everything will fit in the rucksack.

23 November

I spent this morning with Sarah Spinks. She's the daughter of a social worker who was a great help to me when Luke was a baby. We had breakfast by the river. Highlights: two pelicans — seen by both of us — and a jellyfish, which only Sarah saw. 'But it was a nice one, not one of the horrible ones.' Jellyfish, Sarah informs me, are as old as the dinosaurs. ('I'm giving you a lot of facts today.') Then we went to the cinema to see *Matilda*: the book, by Roald Dahl, being one of her all-time favourites.

Sarah is ten. I asked how her mice have been getting along, but unfortunately they are both dead. She's had three altogether: Emily's partner, whose name I can't remember, died first, and was succeeded by Miranda. Initially, Emily and Miranda didn't get on, but eventually they became very attached to one another. Then Emily died, followed only a day or so later by Miranda. The causes of their deaths are unknown, but Sarah has been told that, after a mouse dies, often others will die too, of sorrow. 'So Miranda died of a broken heart, then,' I said. '*Possibly*,' said Sarah. She and her brother James, who is two years younger, are planning to move on to guinea pigs and rabbits next — a pair for each of them — but Sarah wants to wait until she is properly over her mice.

Luke's been away since early Tuesday morning. When he first started going away on camps he would have been about eight. I'd look forward to the break for ages, and then be unable to settle to anything when he went. It was like it is with newborn babies, when they fall asleep during the day, and there are so many chores waiting to be done that you can't do any of them. I'd spend most of the time just lying around, or sleeping.

Last year sometime I began noticing a surge of energy when he was away. I talked to the doctor about it, wondering whether it might be a pointer to something I should do differently when he was here, but she simply saw it as a sign that the worst was behind me. 'You've made my day!' she said. She was right. My energy is returning. I've missed it so badly; I've missed it for so *long*.

I've still taken the weekend off. This is the longest Luke's ever been away; and in case I don't feel quite so chirpy when he gets back, I want to have some special moments to look back on. The temptation is to give myself an unbroken ten days' run of work, but although this is my idea of heaven, it's no longer my body's.

I bought some *weisswurst* sausages yesterday. I'm making a casserole, I suppose you'd call it, of red cabbage and apple, from Stephanie Alexander's new book. It's the second recipe I've made since buying the book and it's as good as the first, which was her version of pork fillets cooked with prunes. That's an old favourite of mine, and it was hard to discipline myself to follow her recipe all the way through rather than fiddling with it, but I'm so glad I did. There was that unmistakable aroma in the kitchen of good French cookery, as I remember it from my lessons with Di Holuigue in Melbourne, when I was first married. Before the kids came along and I started cutting corners to save time. (Not to mention getting sick of cooking.)

Another way of treating myself has been to make a start on Margaret Mead's autobiography, *Blackberry Winter*. I've had in mind to read it since I first heard an extract from it during an afternoon of readings in 1991. I read my favourite part of *A Room of One's Own* — 'What had our mothers been doing, then, that they had no wealth to leave us?' — but the other women made far less conventional choices, as it seemed to me then. We'd each been asked to choose a text which had particular meaning for us.

I can't remember who read from *Blackberry Winter,* but I'm grateful to whoever it was. Here's what Margaret Mead wrote for her daughter Catherine, shortly after she turned seven:

> That I be not a restless ghost
> Who haunts your footsteps as they pass
> Beyond the point where you have left
> Me standing in the newsprung grass,
>
> You must be free to take a path
> Whose end I feel no need to know,
> No irking fever to be sure
> You went where I would have you go.
>
> Those who would fence the future in
> Between two walls of well-laid stones
> But lay a ghost walk for themselves,
> A dreary walk for dusty bones.
>
> So you can go without regret
> Away from this familiar land,
> Leaving your kiss upon my hair
> And all the future in your hands.

It was the last poem she ever wrote.

27 November

I don't know whether it's because I'm working such long hours on the Cottesloe report that I'm hardly aware of Luke being away. There seems to be a definite lessening in contrast between the two states.

It can only mean that he's far less demanding than he used to be. He always needed a steady routine. We, who had prized spontaneity, found out the hard way that sudden changes of plan were too unsettling for Luke. The world to him was an unbearably confusing place and sameness day to day his only anchor in it. When he was away, it gave us the opportunity we craved to cast his rigorous schedule to the winds. But nowadays even mealtimes, which used to be like clockwork, are an irregular business — at least in comparison with what they were. And I can't think of another thing in his day that hasn't got at least a degree of flexibility to it.

29 November

By last night, I was wanting Luke home. There was an empty feeling in the house.

Now that he's back, I can feel that lovely uplift of spirits once again. There's rain forecast. Amazing, on the very eve of summer.

Part Four
Summer

3 December

I finished Jo's report yesterday. I'd been so looking forward to having it done. Once it was finished, I was telling myself, life would be perfect. I would have two leisurely weeks in which to organise our departure for Melbourne. Instead I've shifted seamlessly from worrying frantically about work, and the impossibility of getting finished, to worrying equally frantically about our trip, and being convinced there's not enough time to get ready.

4 December

Carols night at Luke's school. Each year surpasses the last. There are the combined school choirs of Christ Church and St Hilda's, as well as the brass section of the Western Australian Symphony Orchestra. The service is unmissable. I mark it down in my diary a year ahead each year. Sue comes too: it's the one get-together, apart from our birthdays, that we never cancel. She, Luke and I sing our heads off.

We came away afterwards this evening speechless with remembered pleasure. The little boys have their own separate small choir, which sings at weddings throughout the year. They sang a carol by Robert Herrick. I was familiar only with his love poems, 'Upon Julia's Clothes' being my favourite.

> When as in silks my *Julia* goes,
> Then, then (me thinks) how sweetly
>   flowes
> That liquefaction of her clothes.
>
> Next, when I cast mine eyes and see
> That brave Vibration each way free;
> O how that glittering taketh me!

Given this, it was a surprise to me — though I suppose it shouldn't have been, since he was a seventeenth-century poet — that he wrote sacred verse as well. The little boys' voices, piping and hesitant, had moments of soaring certainty. 'Give glory to the day,' they sang.

Give glory to the day.

6 December

Anna's daughter, Gaby, had her baby at eleven minutes past eleven this morning. A boy. He weighed six pounds eight ounces. She and Ian (her husband) haven't decided on a name yet.

You can never tell with babies. Gaby's wasn't due until just before Christmas, so I thought I was allowing plenty of time by having us arrive on the fifteenth. First babies are generally late, after all. (Mark was three weeks overdue.) The plan was that we'd be there in time to look after Laurie's parents, should there be any need, so that Anna would be free to help Gaby as much as she wanted. Now Gaby and the baby will be home from hospital by the time we get there. (Not that I'm sorry, I must say, to have all that behind us.)

10·December

It's Tuesday morning. We leave for Melbourne on Saturday night. There is so much to do, with us all leaving the house together. Claire from over the road is coming in for three weeks, and then Mark will be back, because he has to start university early.

Claire's younger brother and sister will be in charge of the watering. I'm worried about the new plants we've put in this year, and the little lime tree we transplanted, because they start to droop after only a day or so; and even if Alan and Elisa manage to remember everything, I'm sure Mark won't. A whole patch of dichondra and violets which the sprinkler wasn't reaching has dried out almost to the point where they can't be revived. The position is fine — the dappled shade under the pomegranate and the orange tree is ideal — but the watering needs to be constant.

I've got a couple of notes to do for Jo, and

then I can clean up the office. Laurie and I straightened up the rest of the house at the weekend, and I showed Claire round on Sunday afternoon. She is a musician, a tuba player. We've listened to her practising for five years, and in that time we've gone from struggling scales to orchestral pieces which linger on the air. Claire is sixteen. As soon as Mark gets back she'll be off to a National Youth Orchestra summer camp in Melbourne.

Despite being a bit breathless, and feeling that I'll never be ready enough to leave, I'm looking forward to our holiday. We haven't been back as a family since Luke was eighteen months. We've taken it in turns to go since then.

Somehow it was easier to struggle along here on our own. Seeing our families face-to-face became impossibly hard. Everyone wanted to convince us — and themselves — that there was nothing wrong with Luke. Laurie found this comforting, but to me it was less than useless. So every few years he would take the boys back, or sometimes just Luke, to give me a break. Mark and I loved having time alone together. As soon as he was old enough, Mark started going on his own; and sometimes I did that too. Whichever way we worked it, staying in Melbourne was a welcome respite for Laurie, Mark and me, because ordinary life went on there. Each of us could play at being part of it.

What I am looking forward to:

(1) Not being responsible for the household. Not being in charge of cooking or cleaning or washing or ironing.

(2) Going for lots of walks.

(3) Cooler weather.

(4) Going swimming regularly.

(5) Wandering through Carlton.

I want to get to know Carlton again. It was on my beat as a student, but it's changed a lot since then. I lose my way now.

11 December

There has been light rain, on and off, all day. Hard to imagine in December! I'll look back on this diary and think that I must have dreamed it. What if the year we escape the heat by running away to Melbourne turns out to be the wettest summer on record?

I feel as though I haven't been alone with myself for months. What is Melbourne going to be like, in a crowded Italian household?

We'll be staying with Laurie's parents. Papà and Mamma, Laurie and I call them; to the children they are Nonno and Nonna. Anna drops by after work most evenings, and when her older daughter, Michelle, is visiting from Sydney, she comes too. This year Michelle is bringing her boyfriend along. They'll stay with Anna in the apartment she bought after her husband died; but when they're not spending time at Gaby's house, to help her and Ian with the baby, they'll be at Papà and Mamma's as well.

There's a lot of coming and going, most of it haphazard. The only permanent fixtures are the expedition to the Victoria Markets on Saturday morning for the week's food shopping, and Sunday lunch. Everyone comes on Sunday at one and stays all afternoon. There's usually a drive to Carlton for ice-cream. (Mark lived for this outing when he was little.)

13 December

I rang Judy in London. I still haven't replied to her letter and I thought she might worry if she didn't hear from me soon. She's just been to Zurich with Tim. It's hard to believe they've been married for so long. Nearly fifteen years it must be. Only eleven less than Laurie and me, though at first we felt like an old married couple by comparison. When last she wrote, they were going to Paris for three nights, to look at works by Bonnard, on whom Tim is writing a book: 'I always love it — seeing art with Tim in foreign places, a great privilege,' she said then.

Judy is a writer. Her specialty is short fiction, though for years now she's been trying to publish a novel. She has no trouble getting her short stories into print but has had no success with her novels or novellas. She's less depressed than she was about it. I so admire her fortitude in pegging on without the recognition she deserves. There's no doubt about the quality of the work, but there are times when she worries whether she'll ever get a book published.

She asked whether I was finding it hard, Gaby having her baby. She is the *one* person to have asked me. Maybe years ago I confessed to her my jealousy of other women with their perfect babies: three, four, even five of them, when I'd only ever asked for two. What is so special about a lifelong friendship is the asking, and answering, of a question like this.

I know I have put effort into being thrilled, but I also know I *am* thrilled. I want to enjoy being a great-aunt to the full. I have friends who are already grandmothers. Marilyn, at my Thursday morning class, has seven grandchildren, and she's only a year or so older than I am.

I don't know what it will be like when I actually see the baby.

16 December. Melbourne.

The first thing that strikes you is the light. The daylight lasts far longer. You can go for a walk as late as eight in the evening, and still return before dark. The summer solstice is only a few days from now.

But the light is also softer, greyer. It's differently angled. I can't tell what time it is without checking a clock.

17 December

We arrived in time for Sunday lunch. Whether it was the midnight flight, or the rush to get ready in time before we left, we were all tired. The boys and Laurie seem to have slept it off, but I'm feeling worse today than I have all week. I took Luke into town this morning to choose his Christmas presents. Somehow it's better for him when he knows exactly what he's looking forward to.

The tram ride itself was marvellous — we both love trams — but the shopping was hard, with the department stores being so much bigger than we are accustomed to. By the time we got home I felt as though I'd walked into a wall of tiredness. Even though the city wasn't very crowded, it was difficult moving around with Luke; and we seemed to be trekking for miles along the internal walkways between the various shops. I had to hold his hand the whole time because he found it all so confusing. Walking hand-in-hand with a young man of nearly seventeen, who towers over me, I felt old, and out-of-place.

The truth is that, since Luke was little, I've never found Christmas an easy time.

18 December

The place where you are to spend a holiday generally feels unfamiliar for days before it becomes 'home'. Here, that's not so. The strangeness evaporates as soon as you walk into the kitchen and put down your bags. Yesterday, Laurie's mother said of Luke: '*È proprio in casa sua,*' meaning that he's truly at home here. It matters enormously to her.

Her house would not have been considered large by late Victorian standards, and there is at least one in the street that is bigger, but it has large rooms, with high ceilings, and it swallows up the four of us without a murmur. It has iron lace on the front verandah, and a long central corridor. Mark sleeps in the sitting room at the front, which is normally kept for visitors, and Luke has the little study at the back. Laurie and I have our own room, and I use the dining room to write in.

The wide carpeted corridor was where three-year-old Mark chose to stage his protests about Luke's birth. The first involved strewing my sanitary napkins from one end to the other: a shameful sight in this conservative household; and all the more embarrassing because it was my father-in-law who found them. Mark's next demonstration was secretly to disembowel a small fluffy toy that Luke had been given and lay the pieces out neatly in the same place. I was beginning to panic when Judy unexpectedly rang. The second of five children, she had vivid memories of her brothers' reactions to each new arrival: 'Peeing on walls was the *least* of it, Mum says.' I stopped worrying about Mark.

Papà and Mamma spent many years decorating this house. It is in older-style Italian taste, with strong dark colours, which happen to be appropriate to the period, and the furniture in the formal rooms is antique and highly polished. The garden is much simpler than it was when Laurie and I began it for them, before we moved to Perth. The vigorous, water-seeking plants which we recklessly favoured in those days, before we knew what it was to have a house of our own to maintain, have all been pulled out. Now there are lots of *Impatiens* varieties in the front yard, all grown to the size of small shrubs because plants will do *anything* for Laurie's mother. They look colourful, but their main job is to conceal the tomato plants which she has hidden away in corners.

I found a sinewy tendril of wisteria (one of our contributions, long since pulled out — root and branch, as we thought), sneaking its way up the verandah post, and pointed it out before I could stop myself. 'Him again!' Mamma said, and headed straight for it. (Unwanted things about the house are always *lui*. She called our dishwasher 'him' for years before she got used to it; and until then would compete with it for speed and cleanliness. The dishwasher always lost.)

In the back garden, there are tomato plants in tubs everywhere, together with many different green-leaved salad vegetables. Of these, rocket is the only one I recognise. Mamma's summer salads can contain as many as six varieties of leaves, together with freshly picked tomatoes. (One particularly hearty plant is growing in the perforated blue plastic tub of an old Hoover washing machine.) Grated carrot, sliced celery, and cucumber may be added as well, but these have to be bought at the markets. On the back verandah are orchids, rescued from bins in the back lane. The orchids love her for it. They flower more profusely than in any florist's. On an open verandah in the Melbourne winter.

Mark's had his hair cut at a salon in Toorak Road. He says he's never before in his life felt so intimidated, for so long. But he needs to blend into the Chapel Street scene.

 19 December

I can't believe I haven't mentioned Gaby's baby yet! She and Ian managed to come for lunch on the day we arrived, so we saw him when he was only nine days old. He has a shock of long, blond hair. I think his complexion will be olive. It's impossible to tell for certain because he's still recovering from jaundice. Anna and I discuss his every feature endlessly, like the granny and great-aunt that we are. He has a determined little chin, and we think he is going to be strong-willed. Blue eyes, like Mark's.

20 December

Mark and I spent yesterday in Carlton together. We went to an exhibition of architectural photographs by Mark Strizic, dating from the 1950s and 1960s. They give a precise sense of the hope and innocence of those early post-war years. Growing up in Melbourne then, one took for granted the emphasis on the nuclear family (actually featured, in the persons of two parents with a boy and a girl, in some of the photos), and the supposition that a solid (yet light, airy and 'modern') foundation was being constructed for the future. As well as the new domestic housing and municipal buildings of the period, the photographs show the Southern Cross Hotel (now a car park), and the Gas and Fuel Corporation building (at present being demolished). The Ceylon Tea Rooms, too, an old haunt of my mother's and mine, long gone.

We had breakfast at Brunetti's, and lunch at a Japanese restaurant in Grattan Street. (I'm beginning to find my way again.) Mark wanted to see Melbourne University, so we walked through the grounds, though they are a depressing sight to a student of thirty years ago. Almost every open space is now occupied. Even the Law building and the Old Arts building, both nineteenth-century Victorian Gothic structures, are tightly boxed in. We walked back down Cardigan Street into town, and picked an elegant two-storey house for sale in Argyll Place to be our Melbourne pied-à-terre.

He's heading to Sydney next week. I'm pleased to have had this time with him, in surroundings that I knew before he was born.

But I'd forgotten how changeable the weather can be! In the space of one day, we had rain, biting cold winds, and spells of warm sunshine. All in all, though, we're revelling in the mild weather. I'm wearing a woolly cardigan as I write this.

21 December

Last night was a strain. Laurie, Luke and I went to Pizza Hut with my brother Don, his wife, and their two boys. Benjamin and Daniel are nine and seven now, beautiful, graceful children. Don and Carroll are about to celebrate their tenth wedding anniversary.

We felt we'd woken up, Laurie and I, after seventeen years' sleep, to find that the world has kept on spinning. People like my brother have gone on falling in love, and getting married, and having children. The world may have stopped, for us, when Luke was born, but it didn't stop for everyone else. Meeting our families as a couple again, after many years of coming here separately, is making us both feel old and tired. It's hard — in fact it's impossible — to pick up the pieces of our former life.

A good moment, though, in the car park at the end. Ben flung himself at Luke to say goodbye. His head is not even at Luke's waist: it was Luke's legs that he hugged, but he did it with such passion, and held on so tight. Luke gradually became aware that something was happening somewhere in the region of his knees. Like a friendly giant, he reached down and patted Ben consolingly. (We won't be able to see them again this trip, because they're flying out on Sunday to spend Christmas in New Zealand with Carroll's family.)

Laurie, Luke and I strolled back through the oldest part of Prahran. Tiny, single-fronted mid-Victorian cottages, some of them wooden, most of them painted cream. A corner pub dating from the same period. Only a few years later, when the discovery of gold began to transform Melbourne into a boom town, the hotels would be built on main roads, with wide ironwork verandahs. But this pub could have been on an English village street.

22 December

The last time we were all here for Christmas, I was pregnant with Luke. Mark played all day on the beach with his cousins. The worst thing that could happen to him was dropping his ice-cream cone.

We went to Carols by Candlelight in the local park. Michelle and Gaby came too. Christmas 1979. The glowing memory of that night is Laurie's, not mine. I was hot and bothered and sick of being pregnant.

'It was a balmy night, not hot like Perth. The sky so clear. It was like being in an amphitheatre, people sitting on the slopes. The candles. I remember thinking how good life had been to us. We had Mark; and there was the new baby coming. How promising it looked to be. I wondered what the new decade would bring.'

Ten years later, on the eve of another decade, he told me how he'd felt. It was his last recollection of the old country. Of the world where we used to live.

23 December

The roast lamb we ate yesterday had been marinated overnight in olive oil, in a pyrex dish, with slivers of rosemary and garlic inserted near the bone. Mamma cooked it in the same deep oval dish. Beforehand, she had made tagliatelle from scratch, and three sauces: bolognese, pesto, and melted butter and parmesan. With the lamb, there was a *timballo* of silver beet, Italian parsley, ricotta, eggs, parmesan, flour and rosemary — her own invention — together with roast vegetables, and a salad of French beans. This she regards as a simple meal, because she's marshalling her resources for a major effort on Christmas Day.

Her name is Argilde, or Gilda for short, and it identifies her as coming from the region of the Po Valley in northern Italy. The province of Parma, on whose edge she was born, in the lowest foothills of the Apennines, is famous for its cooks, but she is outstanding, even in their company. In the 1920s, as a farm girl of thirteen, she was sent south to work, because her family was large and she was one of the eldest. She had been engaged as a cleaning maid by the family of a prominent lawyer in Palermo, and it was her good fortune that they taught her to cook.

When I ask her what her childhood was like, the only feeling she can put into words is fear. Fear of making a mistake and being called stupid, or worse. Fear of not doing a good job. She woke in the morning to it, she says, and it was the last thing she knew at night. When I watch her, at eighty-two, unable to sit still, always cooking and cleaning, I think of a pattern built up over more than seventy years and not to be relinquished now.

Life in service, young as she was, was better than life on the farm. Recipes dating from the eighteenth and nineteenth centuries were a tradition in the lawyer's house. She learned them from the elder daughter, who was in charge of the kitchen, and who saw how bright she was, and let her help. In this way, Argilde slowly added to her mother's northern repertoire the high baroque cuisine of the warmer south, as interpreted by aristocratic households over the preceding two hundred years.

It's the haute cuisine of Sicily which Giuseppe Tomasi di Lampedusa depicts in *The Leopard*, describing the banquet at Donnafugata, where the delectable Angelica is introduced to her new family:

> the aspect of those monumental dishes of macaroni was worthy of the quivers of admiration they evoked. The burnished gold of the crusts, the fragrance of cinnamon and sugar they exuded, were but preludes to the delights released from the interior when the knife broke the crust; first came a spice-laden haze, then chicken livers, hard-boiled eggs, sliced ham,

chicken and truffles in masses of piping hot, glistening macaroni, to which the meat juice gave an exquisite hue of suède.

The first dish Mamma learned, she told me yesterday, was *aglassato*, simple but very fine, and not to be found in any cookbook today. You truss a piece of silverside, or Scotch fillet — I've even done it with lamb shanks — and put it in a saucepan with chopped onions, a chopped tomato or two, and a bit of shredded chilli to sharpen the flavour. Salt and pepper. A good swirl of olive oil. Fill the saucepan up with water, covering the meat and a bit more, and then let it boil right down until the water has evaporated. When only the oil is left, *sauter* the meat to finish, turning it over and over in the hot oil until it is thoroughly brown. The mush of onion and tomato provides the sauce to serve it with.

The preparations for Christmas Day were under way early this morning. They began with the *melanzane*, which were degorged and then dried in the sun. To these were added fried zucchini and mushrooms, all for the *lasagne*, which is being made in two versions: one with meat, and one, for the vegetarian grandchildren, without. The meat sauce, made with pulped tomatoes from the markets, bottled every February when they're ripest, has turned out too acidic for Mamma's taste. She's tried every remedy, from sugar to bicarbonate of soda, as well as extra salt, but is still not satisfied. Between the sheets of pasta, the acidity will probably be disguised, but the fact of it still rankles.

While the sauce was cooking, she made the pasta dough, laying the sheets out on the kitchen table to dry. Then work began on the *arancine*: big, orange-shaped balls of sticky rice, rolled in breadcrumbs and deep fried, with a mixture of mozzarella and bolognese sauce at their centre. Other people's *arancine* — they're also called *supplì* — are no more than a pale imitation of hers. She makes them with rìsotto rather than plain boiled rice, and they're probably her most famous specialty.

The outbreak of vegetarianism amongst the grandchildren was a blow from which we thought she'd never recover. For a while, she lost her confidence. But slowly, and much assisted by the specialist cookery programmes on SBS television, she began to rally. She had only to see a dish prepared, to be able to reproduce it. Spinach and ricotta rissoles from the Abruzzi region, featured in Claudia Roden's series on the Mediterr-anean, were her earliest success. They survive today in her *timballo*.

24 December

All over the world, I suppose, there are women crying in toilets on Christmas Eve. I can't be the only one.

30 December

Laurie's mother says that this has been a *reasonable* year. Better than last, in fact, in terms of health; and health is her sole criterion now. She will be eighty-three in a fortnight's time; Papà turns eighty-seven in April. They both laugh. *So many years!*

I'm managing to get quite a bit of reading done during the day, when I'm home, but once it's dark it's not possible, because the only good lighting is in the family room, where the television set is. I end up watching it — or rather, talking over the top of it — the way everyone else does.

31 December

In any Italian family, solitude is hard to come by. Too much, perhaps, has been made of the fact that the language has no expression for 'loneliness'; but it is nevertheless true that going off by yourself is taken to mean that you must be sickening for something. Luckily, when Mark was here, I got into the habit of sitting in one of the big armchairs in his room, and reading. I've kept it up since he left, and while it's thought odd, at least I'm not deemed antisocial. (Or ill.)

Living in a household which is not your own, even one as welcoming as this, is wearing. I go out for coffee on my own, either at one of the local shops, or by catching a tram to Carlton. I take the newspaper and a book or two. It's a very pleasant interlude, but it's not like home. (When I am in Perth, contrariwise, it's a quiet hour in a Melbourne coffee shop that I crave, with the traffic rushing past, and city life about me.)

This morning, I met Mum in town. We went to the National Gallery of Victoria for the Assyrian exhibition, and then to Carlton, where I bought two dozen Italian pastries for lunch tomorrow. (Laurie's mother has been cooking all day.)

2 January

Yesterday the house was full of all the members of Laurie's family, with additional friends of theirs dropping by to visit: friends who may know of Luke, but have never met him; who have to be introduced to him. They have to work out in an instant how to address him; they have to decide how long to let him go on once he's launched into one of the monologues which are his attempt at adult conversation. The extent to which he relies on us to smooth his path is far more obvious here.

We can measure our loss minutely, we can measure it exactly, by the energy of our friends and relatives who haven't had to go through this. Luke is about to be seventeen, but fifteen is the number which keeps recurring in my dreams. Fifteen years ago I stopped being frightened and began to be sad.

7 January

I'm on the train to Ballarat, to stay with Jude
and Satch at Clunes.

Between places.

8 January. Clunes.

The stars last night were piercingly bright, and
so many! The whole black night was finely
powdered with sharp points of light. The skies
of my childhood, momentarily restored.

Jude and Satch are renting this property for
a year while they develop their own block
nearer the town. They have a modern
weatherboard house, with three bedrooms,
set on thirteen hectares of bush next to
Mount Beckworth. A winter creek runs
round the edge, though naturally it's dry at
present. Since they left Perth five years ago
to settle here, they've spent most of their
time studying: environmental courses and
plant management; and they now have an
advisory and design business of their own.
They also grow plants to sell at the weekend
markets at Maryborough, about thirty
kilometres to the north.

Jude took me for a tour of the cleared part of the property this morning. (The rest is given over to agistment for a neighbour's sheep.) What it's like, to take a walk with someone who can identify every grass and bird!

I found paw marks in the mud at the edge of their dam. There are apparently six kangaroos on the property, and two have joeys in their pouches at the moment.

The flourless chocolate cake from Brown's in Malvern Road has gone down a treat. I must remember to take one back to Perth for Mark.

15 January. Melbourne.

Riding the tram to town, in blazing sunshine. 'It's like Perth!' I think to myself; and suddenly I'm bereft. Passing the Shrine on St Kilda Road, and aching to be home.

16 January

I managed to squeeze in a coffee with Mum this morning, even though she was due to take Luke out for morning tea. She had to be put off earlier, when the weather got too hot.

We've had two hot spells; one over Christmas and one last week. The temperature reaches Perth heights, 'around the old century mark' (as they say here), but the air is humid and close: less open and breezy than in Perth, so it feels suffocating. The heat only lasts for two or three days. After that the thunderstorms blow in from South Australia, and the weather cools down, sometimes within the hour.

17 January

I'm writing this in one of the local coffee shops. There's a cluster of them nearby. The most famous, and justly so, is Café Latte, but it's closed for the holidays. My next favourite has excellent coffee, and that's where I am now. It's won out, by a narrow margin, over the bakery two doors along, which has the best cakes.

I'm longing to be back in my own home, with my books around me. Ten days to go. I wonder how the children have been going with the watering. I wonder if anything has died. The heat there, by all accounts, has been scorching. The dichondra and the little violets may not have survived. The pomegranate and the climbing roses don't protect them from the morning sun. I'm also worrying about the little lime tree. If it gets through this summer, it should be all right by next, when it will have had a chance to dig in.

18 January

Yesterday was a good day. I met my friend, Jenny, and we went shopping for fabric. She likes my knitted grey wrap, and wants to copy it, so we planned an expedition.

Jenny is Jenny Pausacker, the children's author. At least, she's so far written children's books, but her present project is an historical novel about the women's movement, so that's a new departure.

At her house a fortnight ago, when we last got together, it was daunting to see the two long shelves of her published works: one for the major books, and one for the teen romances she turns out more quickly, under various assumed names supplied by her friends. This is how she keeps enough money coming in to be able to write on a full-time basis. 'A pen for hire' is what she says she is; and somehow she manages it, and manages not to lose sight of the serious work while pursuing the work that pays. She and I were at school together.

She was surprised at first by my new interest in psychoanalysis. It's being fed by the Carlton bookshops. One of them has a whole wall of psychology books. Jenny, who is utterly singleminded about her writing, sees the possibility of my working as a psychotherapist as a way of earning money to enable me to write. For me it's more the attraction of studying again. It's stretching my mind.

I'd planned to take six weeks off from reading theory, but one look at the bookshops was enough to get me started again. Most of the time, while here, I've been reading popular material, like Anthony Storr's books, which are written to be accessible to a general readership. They're none the less challenging for that. But the high theory, as it's called, and especially the work of Jacques Lacan and his interpreters, is luring me on.

So I've read little else, apart from Jenny's latest book, *Getting Somewhere*, a new collection of Pauline Kael's critical essays on film (found by Laurie in the local library), and the biography of Angus Wilson which I brought with me from Perth. I was an undergraduate when I read *Anglo-Saxon Attitudes*; and after that I flew through the rest of his novels and short stories. In England, I found a copy of *For Whom the Cloche Tolls* — highly unfashionable at that time — with the original illustrations. I've been meaning for ages to re-read them all, and I'm hoping that the biography (which I've barely begun) will get me started.

The secondhand bookshop on Grattan Street has a number of his works in paperback, including all the collected short stories in a single volume. I have only *The Wrong Set*, and it's disintegrated so totally as to be almost unreadable. These shops are too much of a temptation. I've a suitcase full of books that has to be got past the airport check-in counter.

19 January

Looking at all the lush green gardens makes me determined somehow to get that effect at home, without any added expenditure of water. If I spent a year or so encouraging the large-leafed ivy on the lattice fence at the front, would it grow? It's established itself there, but — sensibly, since it is facing west — it sends its runners into the cool, moist crevices on the inside of the wall. The Brazilian jasmine alongside is braver about the western exposure, but it's such a messy plant when it gets big. It only really looks good in those neat little pots at the nursery, which are irresistible when it's in flower. (Lipstick pink trumpets on winding stems.)

 ## 20 January

When Luke was three, I went to London to stay with Judy and Tim. I spent evenings in Soho wine bars with my friends from Clapham Common; I lunched with Aunty Myrtle in Ealing. All my old haunts. South Molton Street; the hairdresser's (gone) in Wigmore Street. It was more ghostly than I could easily bear, drifting through those cold January squares in search of my former self. Sometimes I felt I was about to catch a glimpse of her, striding through from Bloomsbury in her seventies leather coat.

I was bewildered by the thought that that young woman could be me. Everyone seemed to recognise me as Carolyn; no one thought I was an impostor. Looking back on that trip, years later, it felt as though I had rushed in frenzy from one to another of the friends of my London years. Maybe they could tell me how to get her back.

Here in Melbourne I am again confounded by memories of a younger self. Perhaps it's being here at Christmas time. Perhaps it's the baby.

It's been harder as he's got more lively. My pleasure in him could not be more intense, but my sorrow for what I missed with Luke is growing. (My sorrow for what Luke and I both missed.)

23 January

Luke's birthday. We had a family tea, with a cake from Paterson's in Chapel Street. A strawberry sponge with pink icing:

Michelle's recommendation. Michelle was also born in January, and this was her favourite birthday cake as a child.

One of the things which I'm only just aware of when I'm here, but always miss badly when I go home, is the smell of this household. Not just the cooking smells, which are always present, and always enticing — the first thing you notice coming back from an outing and often from halfway down the street — but the smell of furniture polish in the corridor. The bleach in the bathroom. Clean smells.

Then there's the spiciness of the bay leaves. Laurie's mother keeps branches of dried laurel behind every bedroom door, and in every wardrobe. In the bathrooms, it's lavender. The laurel is a protection against clothing moths. They are the only survivor, at the present day, of all the diseases and household vermin she waged ceaseless war against in her youth. Unfortunately for us, though not for our clothes, the battle cannot be left to this charming remedy. Instead, the main line of defence is *la naftalina:* packets and packets of it. Mothballs and naphthalene flakes occupy every drawer and every shelf. Eyes streaming, Laurie and I searched our bedroom the first night we were here. We reduced the number of packets by about half — thereby crippling the state of the room's defences — but it still reeks. On hot nights, especially, we're unable to sleep for sneezing.

I shan't miss the naphthalene. But it marks the point at which the divide between Mamma's life and mine becomes unbridgeable. Our wardrobes in Perth are full of woollen clothes with holes in.

28 January. Perth.

Glad to be back! The kids have done a marvellous job with the watering. Everything is green, and wildly overgrown.

29 January

Five pelicans overhead, flapping slowly along in the direction of Shenton Park Lake. *Not* a sight you see in suburban Melbourne!

30 January

Sitting on the front verandah this afternoon, planning tomorrow's sortie, I suddenly noticed a large green pomegranate wedged between two branches. It has faint streaks of pink on one side. I counted seven others, though they have not begun to colour yet. It was so encouraging to see them, in the midst of such hot weather!

This is the tree which produces fruit of the richest, most voluptuous red. They last for weeks on wooden platters round the house.

31 January

Six am start again today. I've been watering, raking the verge and weeding out dandelions, so there's nothing to show for my efforts yet. In the long run, though, it will have been worth it.

1 February

Every day there's a new surprise. This morning it was the Virginia creeper outside the boys' rooms. At about this time last year, Laurie pruned back the azoricum jasmine, which is next along the fence, too harshly. The Virginia creeper clearly knew an opportunity when it saw one. It's spread an amazing distance, and is covered with grape-like bunches of green berries.

The newspaper is recommending planting winter annuals now, both seeds and seedlings. I'm wondering whether to try some in the pots that the bulbs didn't come up in. We're also thinking about shrubs for the bare patches out the back. Hydrangeas for under the tree; hibiscus for the exposed places. *Hibiscus syriacus* is what we're after: the famous 'Rose of Sharon'.

The pots with the annuals in could go on the bricks near the back verandah steps. We daren't put anything permanent in that position, because the ants take them over so quickly. When we tried the new bougainvillea there, it was infested within months.

Mark's been assigned to a respiratory ward for his first hospital rotation, but he keeps visiting friends who are on a coronary ward, because they have more interesting patients. 'All ours do is cough. There's only so much you can do with sputum.'

2 February

A green parrot is perched on the kitchen pomegranate tree, carefully selecting seeds from the topmost fruit.

It was very hot last night. At six this morning, the temperature was still 26°. Even the kookaburras on the telephone lines across the street looked annoyed.

When I was in Clunes, Jude and Satch lent me C P Snow's *The Light and the Dark*. There's a passage in it which puts into words how it was for me in Melbourne. A woman holding the baby of her former lover, who has since married someone else, is described as nursing it 'with an envious satisfaction, a satisfaction that ... seemed stronger than envy.' Holding Gaby's baby was like this for me. When you've had a child that's slow, you never again take normal development for granted. You know it for the miracle it is.

Nevertheless I must have been hard to watch.

3 February

A warm, humid night. The air is heavy and wet. A roar of kookaburras in the tree down the lane.

4 February

The Arabian jasmine is in flower. Heavenly scent. Best of all scents.

7 February

When I went out this morning at six, there was a dark grey raincloud overhead. I watched it jealously as I raked and swept. It moved away slowly to the south, leaving us with only a scattering of drops. I felt like running after it.

15 February

It feels elephantine, the weight of household tasks. On holiday, I forget so quickly how they can overwhelm you. It is all very well to believe, as I do, that whatever one does must be centred in everyday life. This is how, in my mind, I've resolved the pull between my own life and the life of the home. But it hasn't solved anything in practice. (Maybe I'm a bit low with my cold.)

The good thing that happened this week was that I was able to collect Jenny's wrap from Kim, the dressmaker. I took the fabric to Kim as soon as I got back. It was ready yesterday, and it's come out very well. We chose a dark magenta knit, with a thin black line running through it, and a hint of brick red. I tried it on before posting it off to Jenny. We are the same size and shape — we were taken for sisters in Melbourne — and we both have grey hair that used to be black, but her complexion is pale, not olive. So the wrap, while it suited me, will look better on her.

Round the side of the house, where Laurie wreaked his devastation last summer, another beneficiary of the azoricum jasmine's misfortune has been the pink pandorea vine, which I thought had died long ago. Its common name is wonga-wonga vine, and I cannot think of one less suitable. Ours is *Pandorea jasminoides*, though it lacks the characteristic deep red throat to its pale, almost crumpled, pink trumpets. Now it's clambering all over the trellis, and its flowers are nodding in at the laundry window. During one of our first summers here, when Laurie was away, I bought both it and *Pandorea pandorana*, and trained them on to the low wire fence we had at the front in those days. Both were transplanted around the side before the wall was built. I caught sight of the white-flowered one up near the top of next door's jacaranda, where it leans over our side fence, a couple of summers ago. Then it had to be cut off, because the tree rats were using it as a freeway, and I haven't seen it since.

18 February

The last few days we've had strong winds, almost as though the equinoctial gales of March are coming early. There are floods up north. This month so far has been much milder than usual. January, apparently, was fiercely hot.

My cold has worsened; and the irony is that the weather is perfect for gardening. I breathe in the balmy air as I venture outside, and am nearly swayed into making a start, before I scuttle back indoors to my bed and my book.

I'm reading *The Diaries of Jane Somers* again. The book impressed me so differently ten years ago. What I noticed then was not the torments of ninety-year-old Maudie Fowler, fighting for her life, or the lassitude of the teenage Kate. I saw only the world of Jane's fashion magazine, *and her clothes*. I pored lovingly over every silk lining, every hidden tuck. I remember especially the incredulity I felt when she turned fifty, and began telling her dressmaker simply to copy past triumphs.

These days I run into Kim with a pair of my favourite trousers, and say, 'Could you do me three more of these?' And my interest is engaged most intensely with Jane Somers herself: with what she lets go of, and what — only partly her choice — she decides to keep. Even the ending, which before I found too bleak, is less unbearable now. Jane, knowing that old age awaits her, and that she will face it alone, is at last attracted by the life of an observer:

I can see through the open door of my bedroom into my big living room. There is the grey linen sofa, immaculate now, and the two yellow chairs. Beyond are the windows where in black panes blur and blend the lights from the street

A stage set! House lights down ... the sudden hush ... the curtain goes up ...

20 February

A red-letter day! Jenny's written from Melbourne. One of the joys of my friendship with her is her long, wry letters. (And she's thrilled with the wrap.)

I was rushing Luke off to school, so that I could get over to Subiaco in time for my morning class, when the letter came. I was able to take it with me and read it over breakfast.

21 February

I get so *tired*. Ria, who came for lunch, says

that she's hanging on for post-menopausal zest to kick in. I couldn't agree more; but in the *meantime* ... Jenny's partner, Nancy, who's in her late fifties, is full of energy now.

The longing for rain. There's been none all the time we were away; and none since. Neighbouring suburbs have had a few drops, at most. Here there's been nothing at all.

I suppose we're in the dog days of summer: of the *calendar* summer, that is.

23 February

The sky is heavily overcast, and there were boisterous, rollicking winds early this morning. It looks, now, as though it might rain. Sebastian is miaowing his way around the kitchen, and lying in wait to be tripped over. He's been fed all his favourite things, but he can't settle, because the weather is uncertain, and he's blaming me.

He's built himself a nest in the kitchen in the space between the sofa and the sideboard. A cushion fell down and he's made a bed of it. We're not supposed to know he's there.

25 February

Outside the air is steaming. The sky is a bowl of high grey-white cloud. Three thousand kilometres to the north-east, a cyclone is moving across the top of the continent. It's hard to believe that something so far away can be having such an immediate effect on our weather. If only it would rain.

27 February

The temperature is in the forties. I've been staying indoors and doing Jo's work, identifying the occupiers of her shops from the time they were first built, which was during the First World War. One was a butcher's for more than fifty years. The other tenancies, while nowhere near as long-standing, were still remarkably stable. A grocery store, which later became a sweet shop. A ladies' hairdresser (Miss Alva Martin). A radio repairman.

Between times, I'm reading the letters of Evelyn Waugh and Nancy Mitford: the two writers whose books give me most pleasure. I'm having to ration myself. At the moment — 1947, I think — Nancy

Mitford is bewailing the difficulty that *Love in a Cold Climate* (called *Diversion* at this point in its life) is giving her. It's the very best of her books, to my mind; it sparkles and runs like a clear clean spring. I can't believe it was so hard to write!

28 February

Luke got back from camp last night looking taller and browner than ever. 'What did you do while I was away, Mum?'

Hard to say, really. I haven't set foot in the garden.

I've been reading, though: Donald Winnicott, the English paediatrician and psychoanalyst. He is emphatic that there is a term to mourning. Eventually it ends, he says, in its own time. I'm elated by his words. I think that this is happening for me with Luke. I think Melbourne was its death throes.

Part Five
Autumn

1 March

Distant cries from the big black parrots which have taken up residence at the cemetery. Watching them strip a tree is an experience. Even small branches come crashing down. They must be close to exhausting the food supply there, because they're now reconnoitring our neighbourhood in huge curving sweeps.

It's been a calm, unhurried, spacious day. I feel we are our own family again, the four of us. In Melbourne we became fragmented.

3 March

Such a sight first thing this morning! Laurie called me to the window to see a bird on the jacaranda outside. He thought it was a kestrel, but its plumage was greyish rather than brown; more like a falcon's. It could have been a grey falcon, since they are known to make forays into suburban areas, and we have Kings Park, as well as the cemetery, close at hand. In its beak was either a wren or, I blush to say it, a rat.

We've never seen a bird of prey so close before. Most remarkable of all, though, was its demeanour. Other birds are constantly on the watch for danger. The only time the falcon flinched was when Gail's car door slammed loudly across the road as she set off for work.

A few short moments after that, it took off, low and leisurely, over the rooftops.

4 March

The black parrots are close by.

5 March

I was first into the pool today. It was like diving into clear green glass. Coming up from my dive, but still below the surface, I saw my reflected hands above me. They were mirrored in the underside of the water.

Is it wishful thinking, or are the days a little cooler? The nights certainly are milder than they have been. The wind is loud at times, and sometimes chill.

The angle of the sun must be lower, though it's not obvious as yet. But those pinkish-grey pigeons keep flying up from the brick walk (where they eat Missy's dog food) and hitting the kitchen windows. The windows are like mirrors to them, I suppose, at this time of year.

6 March

It's rained on other people's suburbs, but not ours. Subiaco got a thunderstorm this evening.

8 March

I think of ours as a green garden, not a
flower garden at all, and yet there are many
plants in flower at present. Both the
common honeysuckles are still flowering.
The roses in pots have battled on valiantly
through the heat, but if I don't cut the
flowers as soon as they are properly in bud,
they burn on the bush without opening. The
Blue Moon has honoured us with a single
specimen, but it was dead before I could
bring it indoors. The iceberg roses,
however, which I dead-headed in a burst of
energy as soon as we got back, are
abundant. They seem unaffected by the sun.

The Japanese pepper is covered in bunches
of tiny pale green balls. They look like buds,
but they must be the beginnings of its
berries. 'Autumn days,' everyone says.
The mornings are mild, even cool, but the
afternoons are hot and humid. The undersides
of the robinia's branches are beginning to be
lit, now, by the afternoon sun: a sure sign
that it is lower in the sky.

There is so much to do in the garden, but I
am too lazy to make a start. I've been
stumping up and down, watering, but that's

about all. The little Virginia creeper I planted at the front is spreading: it's made enviable use of its first summer. The old one round the side continues to grow. Great armfuls sprawling over the fence. The plumbago I pruned back to nothing before Christmas shows no sign, now, of having been touched. It's in rampant flower. I'm planning to bring a bowlful indoors. The flowers and leaves begin to drop almost immediately, but until they do the clouds of pale blue are matchless.

The big news of the day is that Laurie caught the gecko which has been living in our bedroom since last October. It came in on the bottom of my shoe, and it's been under the wardrobe ever since.

9 March

Nancy Mitford, by the time she reached her middle forties, found herself too tired to go out to big functions, just as I do (well, Parisian balls, in her case); and she was exhausted by the Channel crossing every time she went back to England. I felt much encouraged to read this, especially of such a vivacious, energetic person. She still had many books ahead of her: not only her last novel, *Don't Tell Alfred*, but also her greatest works of popular history. Mind you, the fact that she was to die in her sixties, of cancer, casts a pall. (So young!)

10 March

I'd planned a quiet weekend; and then, though there was no reason to, I spent it cooking and cleaning, and getting angry with everyone. These bouts of high energy, followed by deathly weakness, remind me of pregnancy. But there's no baby at the end, now.

I went outside briefly, to give the dichondra some water. It's surviving, but only just. Amid the fallen unripe oranges — a sure sign that the trees are not getting enough water — I found a little Seville orange tree about twenty centimetres high. I'm going to pot it and see what happens. In *Much Depends on Dinner*, Margaret Visser gives emphasis to the unreliable nature of citrus plants in this respect. You cannot tell what variety will grow from seed. Lemons, apparently, evolved quite late, and in just this way.

12 March

When we came home from the movies last night, we were greeted by the perfume of the Caroline jasmine. This is the second year that it has flowered twice. The smell is more cloying now, and there are fewer blossoms.

Today is almost autumnal. The sun's rays are yellower, in contrast to the blazing white light of summer. The temperature is in the mid-twenties, so that I had to put a T-shirt on over my bathers when I drove down to the pool in the car. (This is a Perth definition of autumn.) I did forty lengths, and still didn't want to get out of the water. Then I lay in the sun with a towel over my face. Sunbaking has joined the list of illicit pleasures.

Gillian Robson, a weaver I met in Clunes, has rung to say that my shawl is ready. It should be here in about ten days.

13 March

Lying in bed this morning, looking through the doorway to the kitchen, I could see Luke eating his breakfast. He was bathed in the sunlight which was pouring into the room from the windows behind his back. The sun is too high for this to happen in the summer.

15 March

An overcast sky presses down. The humidity is stultifying. There is 'the *chance* of a shower,' according to the weather forecasters, who have grown cautious of late.

I was out early this morning, before it got too hot, to tackle the McCartney rose which has been amusing itself by trying to put out the eyes of passers-by. (We've had complaints.) You need a suit of armour to be safe while pruning it. Leather gloves are as the finest gossamer. I've tried training it; it won't be trained. There are great branches, lethally armed to the last little leaf, whipping about in the wind.

It was distressing to cut them back. Every one that's removed means the loss of dozens of flowers next spring.

I took the same line with the Albertine, even so. The year before last we got seven pale pink roses from it. That was in its first season after being transplanted from a dark, damp spot where it nearly died, so we had high hopes of it this summer. Unfortunately, it neglected to flower. Drunk on bulb food, it reeled along the fence, flinging out branch after branch, but not a single rose.

The *Gloire de Dijon*, in contrast, gives every impression of having been born to lie on a chaise longue all day. But it has grown a new shoot, which is up to my shoulder. Does this mean it's planning to produce more than three flowers a year?

Two of the freesias in the frangipani pot are sprouting. *Why*? What do I do about it?

The garden is a source of unremitting guilt at the moment. It's not just the state of the verge, which is more sand than grass, our watering not having been anywhere near as efficient as the children's. It's not even the drooping plants, thirsting for rain after more than three months without a drop. I dither about with sprinklers, but they've become like an emergency measure, because the daily expectation is that it *must* rain soon.

16 March

Rain! Only a brief shower — huge drops — but the air is filled with that stinky koala smell of wet eucalypts, even though the nearest large stands of gum trees are streets away, at Kings Park and Karrakatta. The sky is heavily overcast (more rain?). It's late afternoon. Yet I was swimming at lunchtime in the brightest sunshine.

I'm pleased to be swimming again. The pressures in my life are nothing like they were when Luke was little, but there are others. I get anxious about the contract work; and I never feel I'm giving enough time to my friends. Swimming has remained the one thing I do, apart from reading, that I can drown myself in. The massy weight beneath me holds me up, and the water wraps me round like silk.

17 March

Two mild days in a row. Temperature in the mid-twenties again. 'Autumn weather,' everyone says. As for me, I feel as though I am in transit. In fact I dreamed last night that I *was* in transit, in an airport in Florida.

I was one of a group of passengers with time between flights who were allowed to float in a hotel swimming pool, lying in big inflatable saucers made of transparent plastic. I need to get on with Jo's work, but I *cannot* get started. It's been this way for two weeks. Then there's my doubts about becoming a therapist one day. I am despondent at the time the training will take, and the cost of it. The fact that I am supposed to be studying analytical psychology *for pleasure* carries no weight at these moments.

The Cottesloe project is entering a new phase. Now that the list of shops and shopkeepers is established in draft form, I can begin finding out about the people who ran the shops. For a thesis, this would involve reading endless runs of newspapers, but commercially that takes too much time. So I'm in a quandary. I need to tread water in the sources for a while, in a directionless sort of a way. But that means a low rate of return, probably for weeks and weeks, whereas I pride myself on being businesslike.

Then there are the feelings that come seeping through. On Sunday I gave an interview to a student for an essay on women's lives. There I was, talking about Luke, though I hadn't particularly intended to.

Jo and I spent today together. We talked about bad times: about times so hard that, when you look back on them, you don't know how you got through. I wonder if, when Luke was small, I was madder than I thought. It's as though, in that border country between sanity and insanity, you walk for a while on the other side. You spend some time there, in order to get by. To do what needs to be done.

21 March

The plane trees in Claremont are starting to turn; and there's a new hibiscus on Princess Road that looks like a pale grey orchid. I must take a flower to the nursery, to see if they can identify it, as well as a sample of that slimy creeper. It has now taken root under the mandarin tree at the back.

22 March

Warm days, humid nights. The heat, though,

is like an old lion dying: no longer to be feared.

25 March

This morning, for the first time, the washing was still damp when I went out to get it. No more leaving it on the line overnight! And the Virginia creeper round the side, the big one, has one or two yellow leaves. The strelitzia has produced a final flower. In salute to the summer just ending?

27 March

Cold. Jumpers, for the first time. Luke forgot his, despite my repeated reminders. I worried about him, but it warmed up so quickly that I was glad he hadn't worn one, because then I'd have spent the day fretting that he'd not think to take it off. I'm longing for a chance to wear my shawl.

Luke's excited about Easter. Wanted the E. Bunny to bring him money this year. Instead, we agreed that he could get some money from us, rather than extra eggs. Then he got concerned that we'd forget to go to the bank. Finally I had to tell him that I'd *been* to the bank, and the money was ready and waiting in my purse. '... Can I have just a little tiny look in your purse, Mum?'

It's a marvel to me, this interest in money. Six months ago, he couldn't recognise different coins. His teachers worked and worked with him; and now he's converting chocolate eggs into hard cash.

29 March

Heavy, soaking rain. A shriek of birds to greet it. Ominous rolls of thunder in the distance. We've had two storms pass directly overhead since the rain began yesterday afternoon. (For the first time, proper rain.) Bright lightning flashes in the darkening sky, followed immediately by giant thunderclaps with long unfurling codas. It's gone on for most of the night. Early this morning, when it had stopped, I lay in bed, listening to the steady ping of water dropping from the roof on to the metal lid of the water heater outside. How could I ever have been irritated by that sound in the past? Now it's pouring down, the heaviest rain so far. The gutters are overflowing.

Yesterday afternoon, after the first shower, there was a willy wagtail on the verge. A solid little bird, quite stout. I've seen him once before, I think, some weeks ago, but I can't remember ever seeing one before that. I didn't know they existed in Western Australia.

One of the best things about Melbourne was getting my correspondence up to date. I've been rewarded with a steady stream of letters. I want to spend Easter catching up again.

I've begun the next phase of the Cottesloe work, in a preliminary way, by browsing through old issues of the *Civic Centre News*, which the local Council began publishing in 1950. I expected this to be an exercise in innocence; and, indeed, there is an emphasis, especially in those immediate post-war years, on being cheerful at all costs. Children are invited to submit stories, 'funny stories, happy stories, friendly stories ... Or have you a message that you would like to pass on to all our readers? A happy one, a friendly one, a worthwhile message?'

The Argentine ant was beginning to make

its presence felt in the suburbs at this time, and the *Civic Centre News* counselled optimism about this as well. Extensive spraying was under way, using DDT, and there was no doubt that it would be successful. I wish I could go back in time and show them our verge.

But the most striking difference from today is the amount of community activity that was going on in those pre-television years. The number of clubs and societies! There were well over a hundred of them in Cottesloe alone, many of them meeting at the Council chambers. There were balls, even for teenagers, and public parties. Evening lectures on famous composers had regular attendances of four hundred people, at a time when the total circulation of the *Civic Centre News* was no more than three thousand. A full-scale production of Gluck's *Orpheus* was staged in March 1952, at a cost of £1000, sparking plans for 'a choral society of some sort, which could well be the nursery of future Grand Opera.'

There's lots of advice on rats, as well. 'The rat is a very dangerous neighbour to have in any community ... The number of rats in any community is prodigious. *Warfare against Rats* should be continuous.'

30 March

Yesterday the skies were dark. Luke kept thinking it was about to be night, even though the clock said midday. The clock was nowhere near as convincing as the evidence of his eyes.

The house is full of wintry smells. Plums have got very cheap, and I've been stewing some. I've also made plum crumble, and a rice pudding. Both of them are sitting on the stove top. The kitchen is warm and cosy from the cooking.

My new shawl is draped over the sofa in my study, so I can see it as I write. It looks like a stormy red sunset. The fringe is long, and knotted in a special way that's called Tunisian Fringe. I'm having another made, a plain grey one. Gillian has sent me a square of samples to choose from, and needless to say I want them all.

I wonder whether I shall still be wearing these shawls when I am old. Will I then look back at this diary, and say, 'So *that* was the year I bought all those shawls'? Or will I have them spread on my bed by then, to keep the dark away?

It's strange, this getting older. Last weekend I did out my bedroom drawers. How like an old lady's they've become! All the satin chemises have gone, the sexy black panties. I've held on to only one keepsake: the mushroom camisole with the coffee coloured lace that I bought in Melbourne in 1982, when I was so pleased to have my figure back after the boys.

Now, apart from moth-chasers, the drawers are filled with cotton vests for summer, and short-sleeved spencers for winter. Sensible pants. Thick walking socks. Where there used to be things 'for best', there are now tracksuit pants and bathers. Will tweeds be next, after shawls? Not in Perth, certainly — it's too hot — but if I lived in England, say, is that the way I'd go?

31 March

The streets around us are a buzz of frenzied activity, with the rubbish collection due. All the heavy household items have been out for days, and have duly been removed by neighbours to be stored in different garages for a year or two, before making their way out to the roadside again. But everyone left the pruning until the Easter weekend. The piles of branches on the verges are growing by the minute. Secateurs in gloved hands reach over every wall.

The bees are in the Japanese pepper tree.

1 April

My nephews Ben and Dan got their Easter eggs. They've each left a message on the answering machine. Daniel's was a formal thank you, Ben's more like a ransom note. 'We've already sorted them out,' he said, 'and this is going to be *vairy* nice.' Ben has been wearing his hair slicked back since he was eight. He favours sleeveless T-shirts, in combat colours, and is desperate for an earring. He also wants a lava lamp.

4 April

I went shopping for bulbs this morning. I was looking forward to it but it wasn't as much fun as I'd hoped, because they were expensive: more so than last year, I think; and I kept being reminded of how many of last year's hadn't come up.

I'm not planting any in pots. Instead we've extended the outside bed, where the jonquils did well last year. It now reaches as far as the lavender bushes and the lime tree, and finishes at the front gate, with a little extra plot on the other side under the Chinese star jasmine.

I concentrated on scented varieties. I bought three dozen paperwhites and two dozen Erlicheers. Goodness, I hope they come up. I managed to resist the temptation to try something new, until I saw a variety of daffodil I'd not come across before. They are called 'Hoop Petticoat', and they look more like a wildflower than a cultivated species. They are described as 'an enchanting miniature species', *Narcissus bulbocodium*, from Spain. Several varieties occur in the wild; and they are considered by some botanists to deserve classification as a separate genus, *Corbularia*.

5 April

The Washington navels, green a week ago, have turned yellow since the rain.

It's been cool enough to wear a jumper two days running, without passing out from the heat. (Not the shawl, though.) This morning was hot and sunny, warm enough for a swim, but at about two pm the sky got overcast. I've just heard two faint rumbles of thunder.

More thunder, in shorter bursts. I would be pleased to get some rain before I put my bulbs in.

Luke gave Laurie and me a shiny red egg he'd painted at school for Easter. I've put it on a flowered blue enamel stand, and it looks like a Fabergé egg.

This has been a week of energy for me. Next time I feel I'll *never* not be tired, this journal will serve to remind me.

6 April

The sky was black by three yesterday afternoon, and it rained until nightfall. There are high winds this morning.

I forgot to mention that the Chinese star jasmine and the pink pandorea vine have each got a seed pod. When I saw the first one, hanging off the Chinese jasmine, I thought it was a stick insect. It was about the right length, and the same bright acid green. Now there's another, twice as long, on the pandorea. I still didn't know what they were. Then in the gardening section of the paper I found them discussed. You can gather the seeds when the pods burst open and try to grow them.

There's enough honeysuckle, even now, to bring some sprigs indoors; and the strelitzia, if I am not very much mistaken, is about to produce three more flowers.

7 April

A lost sort of morning. An hour at Cottesloe, going through newspaper cuttings. There are five big volumes of them — guard books, they're called — so there's lots to do. The trouble is that the repetitiveness of the material causes me to lose concentration, so it's better to work for a short spell at a time, rather than risk missing something. At the coffee shop afterwards, I felt lonely. 'Am I in the wrong life?' That sort of feeling.

8 April

Yesterday it stayed steamy and hot, despite the rain. *Perfect* weather for planting. The sun came out again very quickly. I made myself go back outside and finish the bulbs. Those I lifted last year I've planted on the sunniest part of the verge, near the red hibiscus. They all look fit and well: bigger than before, and good enough to eat.

It turns out that Robert Herrick was an Anglican clergyman. It's not his religious verse that's the surprise, but the poems to Julia.

9 April

There are magpies everywhere: on the street verges, in the lanes, and on the roads. They reappeared with the rain a week ago. It's not unusual to see a car crawling down the road with a magpie trotting along in front of it, complaining. You'd think they were dodos and didn't have wings.

11 April

After three hot days, a night of rain. This morning it's dark. The summer's gone.

12 April

Wishful thinking! By lunchtime yesterday, when I went swimming, it was warm enough to drive down in my bathers, as usual, with the car windows wide open. Every autumn is an Indian summer, in Perth.

Am I in the Indian summer of my life? I'd like to be. Pomegranate season. There's been mention of a biography that needs to be done, of a woman who was a great benefactor of the University of Western Australia, and who's recently died. It's mine if I want it. After *Approaching Elise*, I swore I'd never attempt another, and I've stuck to that for nearly ten years. Have I forgotten how hard a biography can be? Will it make a difference that the subject is dead? More to the point, is this book meant to be part of my Indian summer, or not? Last night, my dreams were of Italian aunts by marriage, all ordering me about.

13 April

It's been a weekend of mild weather. Clear skies and bright sunshine. These days look freshly laundered. The people in the next street had a party that's gone on for most of the day. In the afternoon they had an Irish band. For hours, while I gardened, with flute and fiddle the musicians played lively jigs which kept me going; then, as the evening closed in, the music grew sombre. Long-drawn laments floated across the lane.

I'm in a hurry to finish the garden because soon I'll be too old to bend and dig. I'll only be able to potter about in an old cotton hat, with old cotton gloves on, pruning a little here and there. (No more climbing on garden chairs to do it.) Lying on the bed for a breather, between bouts of pansy planting, I had one of those moments that you can never *make* happen, of intense, soaring happiness. (Perhaps it was my hormones.)

The school holidays have started. Luke will be going to Bridgetown for six days. The organisers always send the programme out well ahead of time, so that the children have the security of knowing what each day will bring, and the parents too. Luke's been going over his with a fine tooth comb. He's found, not one, but *two* video nights.

15 April

I've planted the winter flowering annuals I bought: the new 'Harbour Lights' viola, which had better turn out to be worth all the fuss that's being made about it; lots of pansies in yellows, oranges and reds — not the dark, velvety ones — and the stock and sweet peas. I put all the violas and pansies around the back steps; but then I watched the sun all day yesterday, and those steps, which are in bright sunshine all day in summer, now get only dappled light, at best, and for a short time. So I've moved the pots to the end of the brick walk, close to the gas meter. This is not what I envisaged at all when I went through the agony of planting them. I'd been trying to thin out the pots on the bricks, and now they're all crowded together again.

The stock and the sweet peas I've put outside the wall, in the bulb beds, where last year's jonquils did so well. (Seven of them are through already!) It's the only place in the garden where I know that there's going to be sunshine in winter. The rows look very neat and proper.

It was always my idea of what made a real gardener: planting annuals. I'm planning to get an old cupboard for the front verandah, to keep my bits and pieces in. (Secateurs. Snail bait. Blue kitchen funnel.)

16 April

Before I left this morning, I put the cat out by the front door. Missy was standing facing us, no more than a metre and a half away, and though she knew there was something happening, she couldn't tell what. Does this mean her sense of smell is going the way of her hearing (and, presumably, sight)? Sebastian, I have to say, hadn't noticed Missy, either. But then he did, and froze starkly in mid-stride. I didn't intervene. I thought it would be good for him to realise that his old enemy is no longer the dog she was. Eventually, Missy tottered off round the back, and the cat went on his way in the opposite direction.

Will Sebastian be able to absorb the mountain of new information this encounter should have provided him with?

17 April

Sue and I went out for her birthday lunch today, nearly a month late. We haven't seen each other, or even had a long talk on the phone, for weeks. Both our schedules have changed, mine with my psychotherapy studies and hers with moving. We're having to redouble our efforts to make time for each other.

We went to the Italian restaurant in Subiaco that we like. It's only been open five months, so everything — effort, presentation — is brand, spanking new. I love it because every word of Italian in the menu is correct, and I don't sit there itching for a blue pencil.

18 April

Luke will be back in two days. When I made a list in my head of the special things I'd wanted to do, it seemed pointless. A box of chocolates, all to myself. Going to the cinema, all on my own. Taking the day off to read. These are things I do anyway. I can't any longer lament that Luke prevents me from leading my own life.

19 April

Last night, in defiance of the continuing hot weather, I made osso buco: the first since last winter. This morning there's mist in the hollow down the road.

22 April

I dreamed last night that Luke was normal. It wasn't that he had suddenly been 'cured'. He was simply our little boy, Luke. (He was much younger, in the dream.) No weight hung heavily on that name.

24 April

Early this morning, coming back from dropping Mark off in West Perth, I saw three very noisy rosellas flying into Kings Park.

Then Luke made the trip to Claremont on his own for the first time. He and I have been practising it, bit by bit, since pedestrian lights were installed at the Bayview Terrace intersection. With that single event, crossing the Stirling Highway has been transformed from an impossible risk into an acceptable one. Driving down behind the bus, with him on it, I was bursting with pride. When he got out, at the right stop, he shouted when he saw me, 'Mum, I made it!' The round trip is now within his grasp.

25 April

I woke up long before anyone else. Laurie was asleep in the lounge room, where he's been watching the European soccer almost every night. I was able to make tea and toast and take it back to bed with me without anyone being any the wiser. The pleasure of it! This is how I would like my life to be: a member of the household without being responsible for the others.

It's four days since Missy's operation, and she's friskier than she's been for ages. The eye irritation which I took her to the vet for turned out to be a tumour under the eyelid; while they were operating they found a bad tooth as well, and so that terrible smell has gone. Looking back, I can see that the night-time barking, which I thought was caused by her deafness, must have been toothache; and the mad rubbing of her head on the front doormat (put down to geriatric doggery) must have been the unbearable itchiness of her eye.

She has to wear a plastic collar, which is shaped like a lampshade. It has impeded her hole digging, but not by much. She scoops up the dirt instead, although it makes her sneeze. The collar has had a more serious effect on her favourite pastime of pressing her nose under the gate in an inviting manner. Many is the towel I've had to supply to the owner of a bleeding dog (labradors especially). The collar keeps getting caught when she tries to snap.

Speed is the essence of this pursuit. She'll either have to wait until the collar is removed, or devise a way of incorporating it into her act. Of course, she doesn't know that it *is* going to be removed. To her, it must be something that happens to you when you let yourself fall asleep at the vet's.

It's a pleasure to see her so lively. She's once again the dog she was three or four years ago. Sebastian will get a shock! (I must be on Missy's side, to say this.)

26 April

I do think the gardening books should warn you that, once you start planting annuals, you won't be able to stop. From a photograph I saw, I suddenly realised that the idea is to put annuals in stepped rows, making use of their graduated heights, with hollyhocks at the back. So now there's a row of hollyhocks against the outside wall under the letter box slit, with a row of foxgloves in front of them, and then the stock and sweet peas from before.

27 April

I prowl the garden, searching for warm spots which will stay that way as the sun gets lower in the sky. Inevitably, they are few. For nearly twenty years, the garden has been cultivated in such a way as to give as much shade as possible. What winter sun there is, is trapped by the brick walk. But I've found a promising spot near the front verandah.

We've just moved a gardenia from there to the back garden, under the robinia, where it should be more sheltered, and in its place we've put a hibiscus: 'Celia', it's called. We went to the nursery together and managed to decide on it without the discussion getting heated, though teeth were gritted at times. It has orange flowers with cream-coloured centres. Against the verandah pillar behind it, I'm going to put the hollyhocks and foxgloves that I couldn't fit outside, as well as some left-over sweet peas and lots of lobelias. 'Blue Streak', they are: mixed blue and white. And there are the freesia bulbs, too, that I've been saving for a rainy day.

28 April

If I'm to maintain what I've done, I need to stop planting now. There's the front garden to be pruned and swept of leaves before winter sets in, and the new beds at the back to be weeded and mulched. These we've made a start on, but no more.

We've planted the lilac-blue Rose of Sharon that we ordered, and there's a spot ready for the pomelo, which hasn't come yet. It is a grapefruit, but a lesser-known one, from South-East Asia, I think. It has the intense scent of citrus blossom, but with a particular added quality of its own that makes me want it.

The other new bed, facing east, has two plants so far: a cassia, in flower, and a 'Cecile Brunner' rose. We've bought the climbing version, but we'll train it as a shrub.

Luke has to be picked up at 1.30, so I'd better get going outside.

29 April

Over the weekend, I read an interview with Lucille Clifton, the black American author. What she says is that, in order to be a poet, she had to give up ignorance. It was the right choice for her, she says, 'because it got me to what I know now.' To be Luke's mother, I had to give up ignorance. And it was worth it, not only for his sake, but because it got *me* to what I know now.

Another thing Lucille Clifton says, that sums things up for me, is this.

> All people, even one's own children, come with baggage. When they're little, you have to help them carry it. But when they grow up, you have to do that difficult thing of setting their baggage down and taking up your own again.

I counted fourteen jonquil spears this morning.

5 May

I dreamed I was pregnant again. I didn't believe the doctor for most of the dream.

(His diagnosis was based on the fact that 'her wrists and hands are swollen'!) By the end of the dream, though, I knew it to be true; and it was hard, on waking, to accept that it wasn't. (My wrists and hands *were* swollen, in fact, as indeed they are most mornings.) I'd even, in the dream, faced up to the fact that the baby might be handicapped. I'd decided I could cope with that. I knew the ropes, after all: I could manage. The baby was going to be a girl.

7 May

The garden is a paradox. Where you would expect to find symptoms of the year's approaching midnight, there are signs instead of wakening. What should be dying, quickens. Even the roses which have not produced buds are putting out long red shoots. The air is wet and warm, and the earth damp. The soil doesn't dry out between waterings any more.

Both yellow hibiscus have huge double flowers, and the lobelias near the front door are studded with pale blue stars. The ivy's spreading. The Washington navels are starting to fall, and I gather them from the ground each morning. (The Sevilles come later. Most of them are still smaller than they will be, and green, but two have started to colour since the last bout of rain.)

The garden reflects the paradox of my own fecundity. My two boys are almost grown up. I won't be having any more children. And yet I dream of pregnancy.

8 May

The cold nights have begun. Everyone's put winter covers on their beds.

10 May

This is the second day we've had of wind and overcast skies. Still no rain. The watering took nearly an hour this afternoon. But it was worth it, because the Hoop Petticoats have started coming through. I counted seven, in among the Iceland poppies. I didn't know what they were for a moment. They have spiky leaves, similar to crocuses', which push their way to the surface separately, like the fingers of a hand buried below.

Jude has arrived at last. She rang the day before yesterday. She's come all the way from Clunes for her brother's wedding; and Satch meanwhile has gone to England, to give away his daughter, who is also getting married. I'm looking forward so much to a day with her, catching up on news.

13 May

Cold days, as well as nights, now. Unseasonable weather, for May. I've rushed to get all my winter jumpers out.

15 May

Luke came last in the Inter-House Cross Country Race at his school. 'It's *catastrophic*,' he said.

Dew on the grass, this morning.

16 May

The robinia lost the first of its foliage in the night. Since then, leaves have been falling silently, several at a time, like light rain. The back garden and the brick walk are strewn pale green and brown.

The future beckons. Gertrude Bell, one of that intrepid band of nineteenth-century women explorers, used to speak of the feeling of exhilaration as she embarked on her first independent journey: 'the gates of the enclosed garden are thrown open, the chain at the entrance of the sanctuary is lowered ... and behold, the immeasurable world.'

There are two half-grown pomegranates on a branch outside the kitchen window, still green, their cheeks pressed close together. Many of the violas I planted in pots are in flower; the pansies, too. They are mostly lemon yellow and cream, and their faces are turned towards the afternoon sun.

Acknowledgements

The author gratefully acknowledges the
following sources:

p 5 Hélène Cixous 'The Author in Truth' in
'Coming to Writing' and Other Essays
(Harvard University Press) 1991; p 43
Elizabeth Jane Howard and Fay Maschler
On Food (Michael Joseph) 1987; p 55 George
Seddon *A Sense of Place* (UWA Press) 1972; p
75 Anthony Thwaite (ed.) *Philip Larkin:
Collected Poems* (Faber) 1988; p 75 Anthony
Thwaite (ed.) *Selected Letters of Philip Larkin
1940–1985* (Faber) 1992; p 78 Walter G
Hazlewood *A Handbook of Trees Shrubs and
Roses* (Angus & Robertson) 1968; p 86-87
Dorothy Wordsworth *The Grasmere Journals*

1800–1803 (Oxford University Press) 1971; p 95 Dylan Thomas *Collected Poems 1934–1952* (JM Dent & Sons) 1977; p 103, 118 Roger Mann *The Ultimate Book of Flowers for Australian Gardeners* (Random House) 1995; pp 148-9 Mrs Maria Harris (née Debenham) transcript of an interview condicted in 1976 by Chris Jeffery for the Battye Library Oral History Programme (OH 116); p 150 Erica Jong *The Devil at Large: Erica Jong on Henry Miller* (Chatto and Windus) 1993; p 152 PJ O'Rourke 'Bird Hunting' in *Age and Guile Beat Youth, Innocence and a Bad Haircut: Twenty-five Years of PJ O'Rourke 1970–1995* Sydney (Picador) 1995; p 160 Margaret Mead *Blackberry Winter*, Peter Smith Publisher, Inc., Gloucester 1989; p 166 Robert Herrick 'Upon Julia's Clothes', HJC Grierson and G Bullough (ed.) *The Oxford Book of Seventeenth Century Verse* (Clarendon) 1958; pp 210, 219-20 Charlotte Mosley (ed.) *The Letters of Nancy Mitford and Evelyn Waugh* (Hodder and Stoughton) 1996; p 211 DW Winnicott 'The Value of Depression' in *Home is Where We Start From: Essays by a Psychoanalyst* (Penguin) 1991.